KITTEN WARS

KITTEN CHAOS

Anna Wilson

Illustrated by Moira Munro

MACMILLAN CHILDREN'S BOOKS

Kitten Wars first published 2010 as *Kitten Smitten* by Macmillan Children's Books

This edition published 2016 by Macmillan Children's Books
an imprint of Pan Macmillan
20 New Wharf Road, London N1 9RR
Associated companies throughout the world
www.panmacmillan.com

ISBN 978-1-5098-0464-1

Text copyright © Anna Wilson 2010
Illustrations copyright © Moira Munro 2010

The right of Anna Wilson and Moira Munro to be identified as the
author and illustrator of this work has been asserted by them
in accordance with the Copyright, Designs and Patents Act 1988.

1 3 5 7 9 8 6 4 2

A CIP catalogue record for this book is available from
the British Library.

Printed and bound by CPI Group (UK) Ltd, Croydon CR0 4YY

For Lucy and Thomas,
who are very happy you've
come back to us, Jet!

KiTTEN WARS

KITTEN CHAOS

Anna Wilson used to edit children's books until she discovered it was much more fun to write them. She took a flying leap from being an editor to being a fully-fledged author in 2008 and has never looked back (except when she has tripped over something). Inspired by her family, friends and pets, she writes funny yet heart-warming novels which are absolutely NOT based on any MORTIFYINGLY EMBARRASSING incidents which have happened to her in the past.★

Anna lives in Bradford on Avon with her husband, two children and an array of pets, including a dog, cats, a tortoise and a pair of extremely noisy ducks.

Books by Anna Wilson

The Parent Problem
The Great Kitten Cake Off

The Pooch Parlour series
The Poodle Problem
The Dotty Dalmatian
The Smug Pug

The Top of the Pups series
The Puppy Plan
Pup Idol
Puppy Power
Puppy Party

The Kitten Chaos series
The Kitten Hunt
Kitten Wars
Kitten Catastrophe

For younger readers
I'm a Chicken, Get Me Out of Here!
Monkey Business
Monkey Madness: The Only Way is Africa!

And for older readers
Summer's Shadow

www.annawilson.co.uk

1

A Change of Heart

First of all, let me get one thing straight. My dad never liked cats. And when I say 'never', I mean 'never ever'. He was the sort of man who would hiss, spit and shout if a cat had the audacity to enter our garden.

'Nasty creatures,' he'd say. 'And they dig up the bulbs and do their business everywhere.'

Not that Dad was much of a gardener, as I was constantly pointing out whenever a cat dared to use one of the plant pots on the patio as a public loo.

'You're not exactly into gardening, Dad, so what does it matter?'

'It matters, Bertie, because I'm never going to

get the chance to be "into gardening", as you put it, if every time I plant so much as a single puny snowdrop, a cat comes along and chucks the bulb over its shoulder and pees in the hole it's left behind.'

I gave Dad my usual response to anything ridiculous that he said: I rolled my eyes. As if cats went around chucking things over their shoulders! Anyone with half an ounce of brain knew that this kind of thing never happened.

Even someone like me, who had once been friends with a cat who talked.

Yes, OK, so now you're thinking *I'm* the loony in the family. Well, that's where you'd be wrong, because I *was* able to talk to this particular cat. Or rather, he was able to talk to me . . . What I mean is, no one else seemed to be able to understand him the way I did. His name was Kaboodle and he was quite a character – and that's putting it mildly. From the day he catapulted into my life to the day he softly padded away, he created nothing short of chaos wherever he went.

But I'm getting ahead of myself here. The thing is, Dad had always disliked cats so much that I had to come up with the brainwave of setting up a pet-sitting service, so that I could at least look after someone else's cat even if I wasn't allowed one of my own. And that's how I met Kaboodle. His owner, Fenella Pinkington (an actress and lover of all things pink) lived opposite us and asked me to look after Kaboodle whenever she was away. In fact, Pinkella (as I called her, but only in my head – I'm not that rude) was my first ever pet-sitting customer. And thanks to Kaboodle trying to *eat* the only other pets I got to look after, she was pretty much my last. So I suppose you'd be forgiven for thinking that my dad must have been right about cats all along and they were nothing but trouble.

Wrong.

As Kaboodle was always fond of telling me, 'You humans will never understand the feline species.'

Even though he seemed to leave disaster in his wake, in the end Kaboodle made sure that Dad and I were much better off than when we'd first met the crafty little cat. Kaboodle turned out to be the friend I needed while my dad was too busy stuck in his dead-end job to pay me much attention, and it has to be said that it was thanks to Kaboodle that Dad eventually landed the job of his dreams: writing plays that actually got performed on a real, live stage!

In fact, Kaboodle and Pinkella became so much a part of our lives that when they decided to move away, Dad had been as sad as I was. Which is possibly why he didn't immediately throw a wobbly about Kaboodle's leaving present: a tiny, fluffy, orange and white kitten. For me. To keep.

So that's how Jaffa came to live with us. Pretty little Jaffa Cake: my very own marmalade cat.

When Kaboodle arrived with the tiny bundle and plonked her down on our front step I held my

breath for so long I nearly stopped breathing altogether.

'I know how much you are going to miss
me,' he drawled airily, while Dad and Pinkella
exchanged their fond farewells. I couldn't help
grinning through my tears. Dear little Kaboodle,
as immodest as ever. 'So I thought you might
appreciate some company. Her name is Perdita
but you will no doubt want to change that . . .'

She was, apart from Kaboodle, of course, the
cutest, most heart-scrunchingly gorgeous kitten I
had ever imagined, let alone actually *seen* in real
life. She looked up at me with her alarmingly clear
light blue eyes and frowned in
a worried sort of way, as if she
knew there might be a pos-
sibility of Dad telling her to
get lost. Those eyes could
melt icebergs, I'm telling you.

In fact they managed to melt something even

more immovable – Dad's heart. Before I could think of any arguments to persuade him to say 'yes' to me having a cat of my own, Pinkella was cooing, 'Isn't it *sweeeeeeet* – Kaboodle's brought you a goodbye present!'

Dad winked at me as if to say, 'What a loony!' and said aloud, 'It's very kind of you, Fenella. Bertie's always wanted a cat of her own. So, Bertie, what are you going to call her?'

'I – sorry, what was that you just said?'

'What are you going to call the kitten Fenella's brought you?' Dad repeated.

I didn't know whether to laugh or start crying again. I felt as though I could do both at once. Kaboodle had well and truly got one over on Dad. He wasn't going to say no to the kitten now he thought it was from Pinkella. I shot her a quick look just to make sure she wasn't about to blow it, but she just smiled.

Could it be that I was really seeing my biggest

dream come true?

I scooped up the little orange ball, whispered a quiet thank you to Kaboodle, thanked Pinkella out loud and carried the fluffy creature indoors while Dad said a final round of farewells to Pinkella.

The first thing I did once I was on my own with the kitten was to lift her up to my face and say softly: 'Welcome to your new home! I hope you and I are going to be friends.'

The kitten stared back at me with those huge, crystal-clear eyes.

I tried again, 'So, Kaboodle said you were related. Said you were called Purr-something? But he was right – I think I'm going to have to change that, I'm afraid. I can't even remember it properly. Do you mind if I choose you a new name?' I remembered how grumpy Kaboodle had been about humans just 'assuming that they could do what they wanted with us felines without asking'.

But the kitten gave only that unnerving

wide-eyed innocent stare as an answer.

I was feeling a bit stupid now. 'I – er – I guess I was thinking that if you and Kaboodle are related, you can probably talk too. I know cats don't talk unless they've got something really important to say, and I know we humans are not that great at being observant, cos Kaboodle was always telling me that . . .' I tailed off. I was babbling now and starting to feel embarrassed as well as stupid. I glanced at the kitten in desperation.

Stare, stare, stare.

'Oh well, I s'pose it's a bit freaky, being taken away from your mum and dumped on a stranger's doorstep. Maybe you'd like something to eat?' A surge of panic hit me as I realized I had no idea what tiny kittens ate. Kaboodle had not exactly given me a list of instructions like the ones Pinkella had when I'd been left in charge of him.

The marmalade bundle gave that worried frown again, then opening her tiny mouth she showed a full set of needle-like teeth and made as if to mew. But no sound came out. It was unbearably sad to look at, as if she were frantically trying to tell me something but just couldn't. It was all there in her eyes: anxiety, and a lost look that tugged at me dreadfully.

I stroked her gently and made soothing noises. 'There, there, little one. Don't worry. You'll be safe with me. I'll get you something nice to eat.'

The front door banged; the kitten and I jumped. She sank her claws into me and clung on while I winced and tried hard not to yelp so I didn't frighten her even more.

Dad burst out laughing when he saw us. 'Ha! Making her mark already, is she?'

I scowled. 'Very funny, Dad. I think she thinks I'm a pincushion.'

'She's cute though, isn't she?' His face crumpled and his eyes went shiny.

My jaw dropped and it had nothing to do with

9

the fact that the kitten was giving me acupuncture. Something weird had happened to Dad. His face had that gooey expression on it that normal people reserve for babies and small furry creatures. No surprise there then, seeing as I was holding a small, furry baby animal. Except that this was DAD, for goodness sake – the same Dad who had always made it quite clear that the day a cat moved in to live with us would be the day he moved out.

'Er – are you feeling OK?' I asked him, finally succeeding in prising the kitten's claws from my skin and settling down in a chair so that I could hold her more comfortably. She immediately leaped from my lap and bounced over to Dad.

He scooped her up in his big square hands and cooed, 'I'm feeling just fine. And how are *you* feeling, little kitty?'

My eyeballs rolled so far back I could almost see the inside of my brain. Great. Dad had gone loony and, as if that wasn't bad enough, I had finally been given a cat of my own only to discover that she preferred my dad to me.

Dad glanced up. 'So, like I said – what are you going to call her? I guess it has to be something to do with her colour. She's really gingery, isn't she? Not many other colours in her fur . . . You know, I think it's quite unusual to get a ginger female. They're normally tomcats. Hey! What about "Ginger Snap"?'

I bristled. Dad was *not* going to name her! 'No way! That's too, er, snappy.' I frowned. 'She's too soft for a name like that.'

'You're right. And anyway, she's more marmalade than ginger, like *Orlando the Marmalade Cat*,' Dad said wistfully. 'I used to love that story.'

'I am *not* calling her Orlando.' My voice rose with irritation. 'Imagine shouting that down the road! Jazz would never let me get away with it.'

'All right. So . . . something orangey,' Dad mused. 'What about Tango?'

11

'Listen,' I said sternly. 'She's *my* kitten – I get to choose the name. Kaboodle said— I mean,' I interrupted myself hastily. 'I – I was thinking of Jaffa Cakes and Jaffa oranges – so maybe just . . . Jaffa?'

'Jaffa,' Dad repeated, trying it for size. 'Yes! I like it.' He laughed and stroked the little kitten's head as she re-emerged from her self-made hidey hole in his elbow. 'I think she likes that too – she's smiling!'

I jumped up and ran over. Her mouth was turned up a bit at the edges. Was she really smiling?

'So, little one, you like the name? Little Jaffa,' I whispered, putting my face close to hers. But however eager I was to hear something, it did not look as though this little kitten was going to talk to me. She wasn't even purring. She was completely silent.

A Change of Heart

*

Dad and I spent the next couple of hours playing with Jaffa, cuddling her and watching her sleep. And she sure liked to sleep. One minute she'd be charging around the living room floor, chasing a bit of string, the next she'd be collapsed in a heap, fast asleep on the spot.

'This beats working any day!' Dad chuckled, as he let Jaffa run up and down his arms. She seemed to have decided that Dad was a giant playground and that his shoulders were the safest place to sit.

I know it sounds weird, but even without being able to talk to her, I could tell she had a completely different personality from Kaboodle. He had been pretty self-contained: the sort of cat who was very sure of himself and absolutely certain that everyone other than him was not worth bothering with. He didn't really need me at all. In fact, it was more like the other way round.

Jaffa, on the other hand, seemed to love cuddles

and attention and couldn't get enough of us – especially Dad. He seemed so besotted, I thought I had better take charge of practicalities, so I brought up the question of Jaffa's food. 'I'll have to go and buy some,' I told him. 'But I've no idea what to get.'

Dad fished in his pocket, took out a tenner and looked at it. 'Wonder how much cat food you get for ten pounds?' He sighed and a flutter of nerves caught in my throat. What if reality was about to sink in? What if Dad was going to say a cat was too expensive to keep or something and tell me to take Jaffa to the Cats' Home?

I needn't have worried. 'Tell you what, I'm not going to get anything done now workwise, so why don't we pop into town to the pet shop and pick up some kitten stuff?'

Yay! My heart surged and my eyes sparkled. A huge grin split my face in two. It looked as though I was a fully fledged pet owner at last.

2
Paws for Thought

It wasn't until we were driving out of our road that I realized I didn't know if it was OK to leave a small kitten on its own.

'Dad, I think you should take me back and I'll stay with Jaffa while you go and get the food and stuff,' I said.

'Come on, what could possibly happen to her?' Dad said. 'We haven't even got a cat flap yet, so she can't exactly go anywhere. And she's far too small to cause any mischief.'

'S'pose so,' I said reluctantly, but somewhere deep in my head a little voice was niggling. After all, Dad and I knew absolutely zilch about kittens.

Jaffa was much smaller than Kaboodle had been when I first met him. Pinkella had told Dad that it looked as though Jaffa's mum had only just weaned her, she was so tiny. And I knew that was true because of what Kaboodle had told me before he left. 'She's too young to go outside on her own,' he had warned me. 'You will have to keep her in for a few more days – a couple of weeks if you can. She needs to get used to her new home.'

'Don't look so worried,' Dad said, glancing across at me while we stopped at some traffic lights. 'I'll find out about a local vet and we'll get her booked in as soon as possible. They'll be bound to have some helpful hints about how to look after such a tiny cat.'

I smiled weakly. Dad was right. And there was always the internet – I'd googled stuff about cats before when I was looking after Kaboodle. Still, I wished I had stayed behind with the kitten. I could have got Jazz to come round to help.

Jazz! My hand flew to my mouth. She would be mad when she discovered I'd been the owner of a brand new kitten for *four whole hours* without calling her. Jazz and I told each other everything. Well, she was my best mate.

I could text her, I decided . . . but then I remembered I'd left my phone on charge in my bedroom.

Dad was concentrating on the road and hadn't noticed my panicky behaviour. He was still talking about finding a vet. 'Fenella didn't mention whether the little thing has had any jabs or been wormed or anything,' he was saying.

'Jabs?' I said anxiously. I was not sure I liked the sound of that. Jabs meant needles. Jaffa was too small to have needles stuck in her! And 'worming', whatever that was, sounded one hundred per cent totally gross.

Dad shot me a kind smile. 'Don't worry. All animals have jabs.'

11

That did *not* make me feel any better.

'Listen, have you got a pen and paper? Why don't you make a list of things we need to get,' Dad said, thankfully changing the subject.

I rummaged in my bag and in amongst the screwed-up sweet papers, iPod headphones and other random stuff that I never got round to sorting out, I found a stub of pencil and a scrap of paper.

'Erm, "Things to Ask Pet Shop Person",' I muttered. Then I scribbled down some questions:

Things to Ask Pet Shop Person

What does a kitten eat?
Does kitten need a bed?
Kitten loo? (!)
Tips on house training etc?

I was soon so absorbed in thinking up things to buy or ask about that I forgot to worry about the vet.

★

We parked right outside the pet shop, Paws for Thought – cheesy name, I know, but what a place! I'd often wished I had an excuse to go in there, as I could see through the window that it was full of wonderful things to buy for the pet I'd never had. (Till now, that is!) Whenever the shop was open the owner put a cute wooden kennel outside, sometimes with a toy puppy in it. The kennel was painted green with pink pawprints all over it and it had this funny little sign beside it which said:

Paws for Thought

Puppy Parking
Mon - Fri 8am - 6pm

No Return Without Treats!

19

It was a bit like the parking signs the town council puts up everywhere to stop people from leaving their cars parked by the side of the road for too long.

From the street you could see into the shop, where there were shelves and shelves of pretty cat and dog bowls, beds, toys, collars and leads (yes, even for cats!), and there was a separate area for food and accessories for smaller pets like rabbits and hamsters. The hamster homes looked more like fairground rides with their brightly coloured tubes and wheels. This place was more enticing to me than any sweet shop. And now I had a real reason to go in to buy something for *my* new and gorgeous kitten!

The moment Dad and I walked in, we were greeted by a small brown dog with a scruffy cheeky face, wagging his tail so enthusiastically that his bottom was wagging too and I wondered with a smile whether he might take off like a small furry helicopter.

'Hello!' said a twinkly-eyed woman standing behind a surface that was covered in pet treats of every size, shape and colour. 'Hey, Sparky! Basket!' she added for the dog's benefit, and pointed at his bed which was pushed up against the cash desk. The dog immediately did as he was told and went to lie down. 'Sorry about that,' the woman said, her grin widening, showing ultra-white shiny teeth. 'He likes to say hello.'

'That's OK,' said Dad before I had a chance to say, 'Sorry, my dad's not a dog fan.'

WHAT? Dad normally *freaked* if a dog came and snuffled around his legs. But now he was grinning back and being charming and polite and asking what breed Sparky was (Border terrier, apparently) and looking, bizarrely, a bit pink in the face. What with the way he was behaving with Jaffa and now this sudden interest in dogs, I was beginning to wonder if I was living in a fantasy dreamworld of my own invention. I pinched myself hard and blinked.

No change: it appeared that everything I was witnessing was actually real.

'We've just acquired a small kitten – a stray,' Dad was saying. 'And, er, this might sound rather silly, but we don't know what sort of equipment we need or what to feed her.'

We? What was all this about 'we'? I stared at Dad suspiciously. And what was wrong with his voice? He sounded all sparkly and chatty. Dad didn't do chatty, unless it was about work. I was about to say something, but then I realized he was very definitely getting his money out, so I quietly pocketed the list I'd made earlier and kept my mouth shut. I would just have to put up with the weird voice and ultra-toothy smiles.

'You could try one of these specialist kitten foods,' the shop owner was saying. 'Tiny kittens need something that's easy to digest.'

I smiled to myself as I remembered Pinkella's ridiculously long list of dos and don'ts for Kaboodle and how he could only have Feline Good, the posh gourmet cat food in sachets.

Dad let out the most ridiculous fake laugh. 'Hahahaha! I know how they feel – get a bit of a gippy tummy myself sometimes!'

I let my face fall into my hands. Oh. My. Word. What on earth was making Dad talk such a load of loony-bin twaddle?

Then I heard another laugh – this time from the pet shop lady. 'Tee hee hee! Yes, it's awful what happens to your indigestion as you get older, isn't it?'

I rolled my eyes and slid away from the two excruciatingly embarrassing adults so that I could take a look around the shop and not have to listen to any more of their weirdo ramblings. I flicked through the leaflets on 'How to house-train your new kitten', and made a mental note to get Dad to buy something called 'litter'. Then I realized there were a couple of hamsters in one of the multicoloured cages in the corner, stuffing their little cheek pouches full of muesli flakes and nuts. I remembered the time Kaboodle had got a taste for Houdini, one of my neighbour's hamsters, and was soon lost in reminiscing and dreaming about what kind of chaos Jaffa might cause.

Then the pet-shop owner's voice cut into my thoughts. 'You do need to think about house-training this little cat of yours.'

I glanced up sharply to see Dad's face cloud in horror. The woman laughed. 'Don't panic! It's not as bad as having a dog, is it, Sparky?'

The dog looked up on hearing his name and his tail was off again, banging against the side of his basket.

'Cats leave their mums pretty well-trained,' she went on. 'But they do get a bit confused when they first arrive in a new place, so she'll need a bit of a helping hand.' She paused. Dad's face went a darker shade of pink. 'Oh, do you mean—?'

The pet-shop lady blushed too. 'Well, I, er – I could pop round and show you – if you like, that is – tee hee hee!'

What?! I scooted back to Dad's side. 'It's fine,' I said firmly, fixing her with a glare. 'We know about that – we need cat litter, right?' Dad and this woman were getting far too friendly for my liking.

Dad stammered, 'Y-yeah. Do we?'

'It says so here,' I tutted, shoving one of the leaflets at him. 'Honestly.' I just wanted to get out of there before Dad asked the woman out or something gross.

The pet-shop lady hurriedly grabbed a large bag of cat litter from a shelf behind her and heaved it on to the counter. From the picture on the packaging it looked like it contained a load of gravel.

'You're quite right,' she said to me, her face tight as though she'd just tasted something nasty. 'Your kitten will probably know how to use this straight away. Very clean animals, cats. Take the leaflet – it explains everything.'

I felt my shoulders relax a bit.

'Of course,' she went on, raising an eyebrow at me, 'once the kitten's big enough to go outside, she'll look for somewhere to do her business where she can scratch something over the mess – say, soil in a flower bed—'

Nooooo! Just what Dad did *not* need reminding of – cats peeing in his plant pots! I started pulling at his sleeve to get him to just pay for everything and leave. But he was still listening to Miss Flirty-pants, who was going into far too much detail. 'You'll know if the kitten has peed as the litter will be a darker colour where she's gone, and of course you'll see if she's pooed.'

Whoa! Information overload! I shot a panicked glance at Dad. He was going to freak, wasn't he?

But he didn't seem fazed at all. He was nodding all the time the woman was speaking, and just staring at her. In fact, I had the strongest suspicion that he hadn't taken in a word of what she'd said.

But *I* had. And now a horrible thought had started to form in my mind: what with all the over-friendly chit-chat between Dad and the pet-shop lady, I realized we had left Jaffa on her own for quite a bit longer than planned. What if she'd had an accident while we were out? I prodded Dad hard in the ribs and finally managed to drag him away.

27

3

Desperate Measures

'Jaffa! Jaff–aaa!' I called as we walked in, lugging sacks of litter and bags of kitten food down the hall. 'Quick, Dad – shut the door! We don't want her to run out into the road.'

Dad closed the front door carefully with one foot, his arms full to overflowing with shopping, and looked around. 'I wonder where she is?' he said. 'I suppose we should have thought of this – the house must be huge to her. We should have kept her in one room while we were out. Like Bex said.'

'Bex?'

'The – er – the pet shop woman. She was called Bex.'

Desperate Measures

When had he found out *that* little bit of information?

But a rustling noise from the kitchen distracted me from asking. There was a thud and a scrabbling sound. I dumped my share of the shopping and rushed in to see Jaffa on the floor, looking very dolefully and, if I wasn't mistaken, accusingly, at me. Then my eyes were drawn to the kitchen table. The scene didn't make sense at first. There were little scatterings of some white grainy stuff on the table and a trail of wet pawprints going in and out of it. The only other items on the table were two dirty mugs, which Dad and I had left there before going out, and the sugar bowl. It was the sugar bowl that was puzzling me the most. I was certain it had been full of sugar earlier because I remembered Dad heaping a spoon and stirring it into his coffee that morning, but now it seemed to be full to overflowing with a strange yellowish liquid that, in my confused state, I thought might possibly have been washing-up liquid.

'Dad? Why did you leave the sugar bowl to soak on the table?' I called.

Dad entered the kitchen. 'I didn't.'

'Watch it!' I called as he nearly stepped on Jaffa, who was skulking near a chair leg.

Dad stopped abruptly in his tracks and teetered backwards, peering round the bags of cat litter as he looked out for the kitten. He couldn't sustain this awkward pose and ended up losing his balance, dropping the sacks and causing Jaffa to rocket across to the other side of the kitchen like a mad March hare to try and hide under one of the fitted cupboards. She got stuck, her little bottom up in the air as she tried to decide whether to squash herself further under or pull herself back out. It reminded me of the Winnie-the-Pooh story I used to love when I was younger, where Pooh gets stuck in Rabbit's doorway. I giggled while Dad scrabbled around to retrieve the bags.

'Thanks for helping,' he said sarcastically. Then: 'What was that you said about the sugar bowl?'

'Oh yes – it's just a bit strange. Look at it,' I said, gesturing vaguely at the bowl while keeping my eyes fixed on my cute little cat, wiggling her bottom in the air.

'OH NO!'

I whirled round. Dad was leaning over the table, holding the sugar bowl out at arm's length, his face contorted with repulsion. 'That is DISGUSTING!' he cried, carefully lowering the bowl back down again.

'What?' I said.

'That!' Dad said, jabbing his finger at the bowl.

'I don't get it,' I said, shaking my head.

Dad shuddered. 'It looks like a case of desperate times calling for extremely desperate measures.' I looked at him blankly. 'Let's just say that your new pet couldn't *quite* wait for us to come back from the shops with a litter tray,' Dad said with a heavy note of irony.

'Wha—? Aargh!' I backed away from the table.

'Cat pee,' Dad said, to emphasize a point already very well made in my opinion.

'OK!' I said irritably. 'What do you expect me to do about it?'

'Well now, let me see . . .' Dad smiled and made a big show of having a think, scratching his head and rubbing his chin, taking his glasses off and giving them a good clean.

'All right – I get it. She's my pet, so I have to clean the cat pee out of the sugar bowl.' Even as I said the words I realized how utterly bizarre they sounded. Who had ever heard of a cat using a sugar bowl as a loo? I gingerly picked up the offending article and then held it underneath as well with my other hand. There was no way I wanted to spill a drop of the stuff. I carefully moved away from the table and started a slow journey to the sink.

Behind me, Dad let out a splutter of laughter.

I whirled round in surprise and succeeded in sloshing a wave of sugared pee solution down the front of my best hoody. 'AARGH! What did you have to do that for?' I yelled.

Dad was bright red in the face, gasping and wheezing with laughter now. He was pointing at me and then at Jaffa who was still squirming under the cupboard, and squeaked something which sounded like, 'Tiny bottom.'

I was not amused.

I put the sugar bowl in the sink and ran out of the room to change my top and wash my hands.

When I came back downstairs, Dad's face had returned to its normal pinky-whitish colour and he had stopped shaking and heaving with hysterical laughter.

'So you've come back down to Planet Normal then?' I said, mustering as much sarcasm as I could.

33

Dad grinned. 'Sorry, but I just couldn't shake this picture I had in my head of – of,' he struggled to maintain control. 'You know, of Jaffa perching over the sugar bowl, her tiny bottom . . . perfectly balanced . . . so as to aim right into the . . .' He tailed off and the wheezing took over again.

My eyes rolled into the back of my head. 'For goodness sake!' I snapped. 'Where is Jaffa, by the way?' I realized I'd left Dad in sole charge while I'd been out of the room, which in his present state was not an entirely sensible idea.

Dad just shook his head, tears running down his face. Useless.

Scrabble, scrabble!

'What was that?' I asked, spinning round to where I thought the sound had come from. It sounded as if it was above my head, but that couldn't have been right.

Scrabble, scrabble, scrabble!

It *was* coming from above my head. I looked up.

Desperate Measures

The only things above me were the ceiling, the light fittings and—

'DAD! She's on top of the cupboards! Quick – stop laughing, for goodness sake – she's stuck! Get a chair or something. DAD!'

Oh, that man was hopeless sometimes. I grabbed a chair and then because I wasn't tall enough to reach the top of the cupboard, I climbed on to the work surface and stretched up to where Jaffa was peeping over the top of the cupboard where we kept the cereals.

'It's OK, Jaffa. I'm here. Just jump!' I said, reaching forward and trying not to fall off.

Those jewel-like eyes just stared and stared. Then Jaffa stretched her mouth alarmingly wide and did that silent mewing thing again.

Dad hiccuped and dried his eyes. 'Bertie, come down. You'll fall—'

Too late. I leaned back too far and slipped off the work surface on to the floor. Picking myself up

35

with stars whirring in front of my eyes, I tried to tell Dad to do something useful and get a stepladder. But before the words were properly formed in my mind there was a soft thud and Jaffa landed on my tummy, walked up to my face and pushed her nose against mine.

How could I be cross with such an adorably cute ball of fluff after that?

'Wow, Jaffa!' I breathed, gently stroking her sticky-uppy fur as she rubbed against my cheek. 'Life sure is going to be interesting with you around the place.'

4

New Kid on the Block

Jaffa kept us busy round the clock for the next couple of days, 'missing' her new litter tray more than once, getting stuck on curtain rails by using the curtains as ladders (Dad nearly lost his sense of humour over that), and falling asleep in the washing machine (only once, thank goodness). That had totally freaked me out. Dad had dumped a load of clothes on her and had been about to switch the machine on, when he'd spotted a small frightened face peering out at him through the door.

It wasn't until the morning of day three that I finally remembered to unplug my mobile from the charger and check my messages. I wasn't that into using it, mainly because now my pet-sitting days were over, no one except Dad and Jazz had the number and Dad had said I wasn't allowed to use it unless it was for emergencies. But Jazz had always ignored that fact and texted me constantly. And she got pretty cheesed off when I didn't respond right away.

So when I finally scrolled through my messages, I felt a sickening lurch of guilt as I saw that I had so many unread ones from Jazz that the inbox was full to bursting. And there were a gazillion voicemail messages from her too. She's going to be seriously mad at me, I thought grimly as I took the plunge and called up her name from my address book.

As usual she answered after the first ring. I dimly wondered whether she walked around with her phone permanently strapped to her ear, but pushed the thought aside and started talking at top speed.

'Hey, Jazz. How're you doing? Really sorry I've not been round this week, but you have *no* idea what's being going on,' I babbled.

But Jazz had already interrupted and was talking at top speed herself. 'Oh yeah? Well, *you've* no idea what's been happening *this* end. It's been, like, totally hectic,' she announced.

Typical. Even in phone conversations Jazz manages to be competitive.

I was relieved she wasn't angry, but that feeling was already being swallowed up by a sense of impending doom. What was she up to now? 'OK, don't tell me,' I said. 'You've just won the National Eurovision Search for a Child Superstar.'

'Duh! You can't be National *and* Eurovision,' said Jazz. 'And anyway, it's got nothing to do with my inevitable rise to fame as a mega popstar singing and dancing act . . .'

For once, I thought.

'. . . *yet* . . .' Jazz added, layering on the suspense.

'What? Oh, listen, you can tell me later. Can you

39

come round?' I said. 'I've got something mega cute to show you.' I tried adding in a bit of suspense myself. 'You are not going to believe it.'

'O-kaay,' Jazz said slowly. 'No need to go all hyper on me. Hey – what do you mean, cute?' she added quickly.

'You'll have to come round and see for yourself,' I said in what I hoped was a tantalizing tone.

Jazz sighed noisily into the receiver. It made my ear tingle. 'All right, I'll be there in five.'

I grinned. Gotcha! I thought. The expression 'curiosity killed the cat' could have been tailormade for Jazz.

While I was waiting for my best friend to arrive, I put down some of the kitten food to try and tempt Jaffa to come out from under the radiator, but she was firmly wedged up against the skirting board and peering out at me with those huge glass-button eyes as if to say, 'If you think I'm moving any time soon, you've got another think coming.' Of course that was only my interpretation, as she still had not uttered a single peep of anything to me.

'Let's put the litter tray by the back door in the utility room,' Dad suggested. 'That way she might eventually get used to the idea that she has to go out to pee, rather than looking for other – receptacles!' His shoulders started shaking with silent laughter.

Great! That little escapade was going to keep Dad amused for weeks, if not months, I could see. He'd probably end up writing it into one of his plays, knowing my luck, then everyone would get to know about it. Why did his sense of humour have to be so pathetic?

'OK,' I said, shooting him an I'm-ignoring-your-childish-behaviour look. 'I suppose when she's had her jabs we could put a cat flap in the back door? Then she can go out into the garden whenever she wants.'

Dad had turned up the volume on his silent laughter and was wheezing and hooting again.

'Oh, for goodness sake!' I snapped.

Luckily the doorbell rang.

'That'll be Jazz,' I said pointedly.

Dad took the hint and went up to his study. I carefully shut the kitchen door behind us, making sure Jaffa was still safely under the radiator. Every day had been like this so far, with Dad and I working together to cover all available entrances and exits as though we were a SWAT team trying to contain a heavily armed criminal. I grimly thought things might be easier if we'd had night-vision goggles, motion detectors and perhaps walkie-talkies to communicate from one doorway to the next. This cat was a serious contender for Cat Burglar of the Year Award, she was so swift and silent.

I opened the front door, my heart still pounding from the covert operation in the kitchen.

'Hi!' Jazz was bouncing up and down on the doorstep, grinning like an overexcited chimpanzee –

one who'd just won the Banana Lottery, by the looks of her.

But I couldn't help it; I started bouncing too, all thoughts of my dad's insanity and my worries of escaping felines immediately forgotten in my eagerness to show off my new kitten. (*MY new kitten!* How cool did that sound?)

'Hi! Come and see this!' I said, flinging out an arm in the direction of the kitchen. I grabbed Jazz by the elbow and propelled her into the house, automatically checking all doors and windows and slamming the front door shut behind her.

'Whoa! What's up?' Jazz hurtled down the hall after me.

I got to the kitchen door then turned and put a finger to my lips. 'You'll scare her if you make too much noise,' I said, my voice low. 'And watch where you put your feet.'

Jazz was shaking her head at me and making a face that quite clearly said, 'You are an out-and-out ultra-stressy nutcase.'

I opened the door a crack and scouted round to make sure Jaffa wasn't going to make a break for it or get squashed. No sign of her directly in my line of vision. I took a deep breath and hissed, 'Ready?' to Jazz. She shrugged and half nodded, so I grabbed her arm again and whizzed her in behind me.

I dropped down on to my hands and knees and gestured to Jazz to do the same. 'Ber-tiiiie!' she wailed. 'What is it with all this Alex Rider rubbish? Get up, can't you? I've got my best black jeans on!'

I pulled down the corners of my mouth in disgust. 'Get a life, Jazz. I want to show you something much better than your stupid jeans. Under here – look.'

Curiosity overcoming her annoyance, Jazz joined me down on the floor and peered under the radiator. A sweet little orange and white face peered worriedly back, the huge unblinking blue eyes flashing with fear and trepidation. My heart swelled so much I thought I might choke.

'Oh. A kitten,' Jazz said, sounding distinctly underwhelmed. 'What's she doing under there?' She reached out and tried to touch Jaffa, but the tiny cat backed away and her face creased up into an expression of such total anxiety that I felt I must look like a monster looming over her like that.

'Hey, maybe we should let her come out in her own time,' I said cautiously.

'Why won't she let me touch her?' Jazz said accusingly. 'What is it with me and cats? First Kaboodle and now this one.'

It was true Kaboodle had never exactly been fond of Jazz, but I couldn't prevent my hackles from rising. I felt incredibly overprotective of my little cat. Trust Jazz to get on the wrong side of Jaffa already.

'I think you've just got to give her time to get used to you. She's a real softie, aren't you, Jaffsie?' I coaxed, pressing my face closer to the floor to make my head level with hers. 'Hey, why don't you come out?' I reached one hand towards her to try and stroke her, to reassure her.

Her eyes widened in alarm as my hand crept to-

wards her and in a sudden streak of bright orange, she shot out from under the radiator like a flame and headed for the util- ity room. Jazz and I scrambled to our feet and scuttled after her. There was nowhere to hide in there, so the kitten threw herself into the air in a wild attempt to shin up on to a cupboard, but she missed her footing and slid back to the floor. I swiftly scooped her up before she could rush at the cupboard again. She must have been a bit dazed from her fall, because she shook her head and blinked and then sat in the palm of my hand and let out another silent mew that seemed to go on for ages, her mouth stretched wide and her whiskers stiff with fear.

Jazz hadn't seemed to notice, however. 'So – can

I hold her, or what? Only, this is getting a bit . . .'
she yawned extravagantly, '. . . *bor-ing*.'

I frowned at Jazz and turned my attention to
the poor little kitten. 'Are you frightened?' I asked
softly.

Jaffa looked up at me. I gasped. 'Did you see
that?' I hissed at Jazz. 'She nodded!'

'Yeah, yeah,' said Jazz, inspecting her chewed-off
nails, painted a petrol-blue today, I noted. 'And she
told me she'd like a plate of tuna washed down with
a saucer of milk. What are you like, Bertie? You
were always going on about that Kaboodle like he
was a human, and now you're doing it with this cat.
Anyone would think you could "talk to the animals",' she crooned in a sing-song voice. 'Where's
she come from anyway? You never said you were
getting a kitten. Does your dad know about this?
Won't he freak?'

'It's OK, Dad knows all about Jaffa,' I said
quietly.

Jazz raised one eyebrow sceptically. 'And what kind of a name is *that*?'

I felt a prickle of annoyance. 'It's like Jaffa Cake or Jaffa oranges – you know? Cos she's orange.' I was not in the mood for one of Jazz's stupid arguments. 'Do you want to know how I got Jaffa or what?'

I went back into the kitchen and Jazz followed, huffing and puffing. I grabbed a packet of chocolate-chip cookies to get her in a better mood, then we drew back a couple of chairs and sat down. I put Jaffa on my lap, where she promptly fell into a deep sleep, and told Jazz the whole story about Pinkella bringing Jaffa round. (I missed out the bit about Kaboodle being in charge of the handover, obviously, as I knew Jazz would just say something along the lines of me being clinically insane.) I burbled on about our trip to Paws for Thought and all the stuff 'Bex' had advised us on, and how weird it was to suddenly have to think of all these things. (I also missed out the bit about Dad batting his eyelashes at 'Bex', as I knew Jazz would never let me forget it.) And I finished by saying that the strangest thing of all was that Cat-Hater Extraordinaire, i.e. Dad, seemed to have fallen head over heels for Jaffa just like that, and hadn't even minded when she'd peed in the sugar bowl.

'When she WHAT?' Jazz said, howling with laughter and causing Jaffa to twitch in her sleep.

I shrugged. 'Yeah, well, I guess she'll take her time getting used to living in a new place.'

'Yes, but the *sugar bowl*?'

'OK, I've had enough of that from Dad,' I said tetchily.

Jazz pulled a face. 'Sor-ree. Anyway, you're not the only one with exciting news, as it happens,' she added, tossing her head airily and crossing her arms, pretending she wasn't bursting to tell me her secret.

I remembered guiltily that Jazz had mentioned

something on the phone earlier. 'Oh, yes – you said. So, er, are you going to tell me about it?' I asked.

Jazz couldn't keep up the cool act any longer. Her eyes flashed and she leaned in towards me, every single one of her gleaming white teeth on show in a maniacal grin.

'A family's moving into Pinkella's house opposite. You're getting new neighbours . . .' She paused for dramatic effect. 'And I know who they are.'

I looked carefully at my friend's flushed face. 'Well, whoever it is, you seem pretty excited about it. Hey! It's not Zeb Acorn from *Summer School Dance Camp*, is it?'

'Are you trying to be funny?' Jazz said darkly. 'Cos it's *so* not working.'

Jazz has watched her DVD of *Summer School Dance Camp* so many times it's a miracle the DVD player doesn't just put it on automatically every time she walks in the room. She knows every word of every song and every tiny variation of every dance move. Oh, and she's totally in *lurve* with Zeb Acorn, one of the actors who stars in it. And by the way she's going to marry him. Although I'm not sure he knows that yet.

I raised an eyebrow at her and said innocently, 'Me? Trying to be funny?'

Jazz inhaled deeply so I cut in fast to prevent one of her tirades about how I didn't appreciate fine music, etc etc, blah-di-blah-di-blah-blah. 'So, who *is* going to move in then?'

Jazz put on her knowing look again and said, 'It's a family. With a boy. He's coming to our school after the holidays. He'll be in Year 9 and he's called Fergus.' She sat back, a look of smug satisfaction spread across her face like a cat who's broken into the fish shop and helped itself to starter, main course and dessert and then scarpered before getting caught.

'Fergus? What kind of a name is *that*?' I said in disgust, echoing Jazz's earlier criticism of 'Jaffa' as a name. Fergus. Sounded like Fungus, like the kind of name you'd give a pet frog, I thought sullenly. And a *boy*? Why couldn't it have been a family with a girl my and Jazz's age? That would've been cool. But a boy? And two years above? I couldn't see what Jazz was so excited about.

'Like you're any good at choosing names,' Jazz sneered. 'Anyway, Mum's met them, cos they came round to see their new house yesterday and Mum and Aleisha were passing, so they said 'hi'. Mum says the boy's really into music!' Jazz squeaked. 'He's in a band, plays guitar *and* sings. Do you reckon they need any backing vocals?'

OK, it was all becoming clear now. Jazz was always on the lookout for a way to further her so far non-existent singing and dancing career. She was hoping Mr New Boy on the Block was going to be her way to fame and fortune.

'It's probably just some gross grungy boy band full of geeks with greasy hair,' I said. 'Don't you think you'd better wait until you meet him before you get so excited?'

Jazz leaped to her feet, her excitement instantly replaced with anger. It was freaky how quickly that girl could switch her moods sometimes.

'You're just jealous that I found out before you did!' she snapped.

'Jealous? Of what? You haven't even met the guy yet, anyway—'

'It's OK, I get it,' Jazz interrupted. She always did that if she knew she was going to lose an argument. 'You're too busy with your new baby. Never mind. I'll see you around.'

She pushed her chair back noisily and made for the door.

'Wait, Jazz!' I called after her, shifting awkwardly so as not to wake the ball of fluff that was still snoozing on my lap. 'Stop! I didn't mean . . .'

I tried to ease Jaffa into my arms without waking her so that I could go after my friend.

But it was too late. She'd slammed the door.

I looked down at Jaffa. 'Seems like a case of "three's a crowd",' I said sadly. I sighed and gently rubbed the kitten's ear.

I couldn't sleep that night. And it wasn't just because I had a skittish kitten careering around my room like a bolt of lightning, chasing shadows, spiders – anything that so much as flickered in the gloom. It was also because I felt totally hollow after Jazz had walked out on me.

I had tried talking to Dad about it after Jazz had gone, but he had given me all the usual guff about, 'You girls are always falling out – one minute you're best of friends, the next minute you're not talking. You'll get over it.' Thanks for nothing, Dad. He didn't give me a chance to tell him about the new neighbours, either. I wondered if he would even care.

I wouldn't have minded if the argument with Jazz had been worth it. But all that huffing and puffing just because some lame boy could sing a few songs? I knew what those school 'bands' were like. There were some acne-fied guys at our school who'd done a gig for the fair last year to raise money for charity. 'The Skulls', they called themselves. Complete ear-splitting, teeth-grinding rubbish. Jazz was off her head if she thought Mr New Boy's band was going to be any different.

I sighed and wriggled around to find a cool patch in the bed. This summer was turning out to be hotter than any I could remember. I was desperate to have the window open, but I didn't dare in case Jaffa got out – and she was already pawing at the glass. I sighed. Poor Jaffa, she was probably as hot as me. Especially with all that fur.

'Jaffa? Jaffsie! Come here, cutie. What are you doing?'

I didn't know why I kept talking to this animal. It wasn't as if she even purred back at me. I carried her back to my bed.

'Hey, little Jaffs, I just don't believe you can't speak to me,' I tried again later, during a moment of quiet when she was sitting on my tummy, her eyes flashing like lamps in the gloom. 'Maybe you can and it's just that I'm still really unobservant.' I hesitated, willing myself to tune into Jaffa's wavelength. 'Maybe you're cross with me for taking you away from your family?' I ventured. 'You know, I didn't ask for Kaboodle to bring you here – I mean, don't get me wrong, I am totally thrilled that you *are* here. It's such a dream come true, I can't tell you.'

Jaffa made a tentative move towards my face as I said this, but thought better of it and sat back down. Then just as it seemed like she might settle down and go to sleep, something caught her eye and she was off again, whirling round the room as though she were being chased by a pack of angry dogs.

I glanced at my alarm clock. Two o'clock! This was no good. I had to get some sleep.

I scooped up the little ginger firework and crept down to the kitchen, shutting her in the utility room, thinking at least she'd have her litter tray in there. Then I tiptoed back up the stairs so as not to wake Dad. I needn't have worried – he was snoring for England as usual.

I snuggled back down and closed my eyes, letting my mind wander aimlessly and at last began to drift off, dreaming that Jaffa was sitting by my ear, whispering to me in a voice that sounded like Kaboodle's: 'Jazz is just jealous. She'll get over it.'

Even in my semi-awake state, I doubted that she would.

5

Pins and Needles

In the end I slept in. I was woken by Dad banging on my door, shouting at me to 'come and help clear up the mess downstairs'. I stomped wearily down in my PJs to find him scrabbling around with a bucket and a mop, a look of despair etched on his face.

'So much for cats being clean creatures,' he muttered. 'She's kicked most of the litter out of the tray. It gets everywhere this stuff – look!' He pointed through the open utility room door to where clumps of cat litter and bits of sodden kitchen roll lay all over the floor.

I went in, tiptoeing over the mess, and grabbed a

dustpan and brush.

'Where is she?' I asked, while I swept the dirty litter into a plastic bag.

'I think she's skulking up there,' Dad answered, pointing to the wash basket on top of the washing machine. 'I'm going to make some coffee. Come and get your breakfast. We're due at the vet's in half an hour.'

I'd forgotten about that. Apparently it was important to get Jaffsie vaccinated as soon as possible.

'Found yourself a comfy bed then!' I said softly, peering into the laundry basket. Jaffa didn't blink; she carried on snoozing in that snuffly kittenish way of hers that sounded almost like snoring. 'Don't go getting in the washing machine again now, will you?'

Dad came up behind me with a steaming mug of coffee. 'Hello, little Jaffa,' he said cheerily, all comments on mess and dirt forgotten, I noticed with relief.

Kitten Wars

Jaffa unfurled from her sleeping position and arched her back in a luxurious stretch and then sat back on her haunches and reached out with her front paws. It was so sweet seeing her behave like a fully grown cat when she was still so small!

'Aah, have you had a lovely sleep then?' Dad twittered, giving her back a little stroke with one finger.

Jaffa blinked at Dad.

'Not very talkative, are we?' Dad went on. 'Come to think of it, Bertie, have you heard her say *anything* yet?'

I stared at him. 'What do you mean, *say* anything?' Had Pinkella known all along that I could talk to Kaboodle? Had she said something to Dad?

Dad looked at me strangely. 'You know – has she mewed or made any cat-like noises, howling or – I don't know, *anything*? It's just she seems very quiet to me. Do you think something's wrong with her?'

Pins and Needles

I breathed again, relieved Dad wasn't talking about actual words. 'Oh, no. I mean, I don't know whether there's anything wrong, but I haven't heard any miaows or anything, no. Maybe we could ask the vet about it later?'

'Yes!' Dad glanced at his watch. 'Blimey – look at the time. Come on Bertie, you have to eat and get dressed now. I'll find a box to put Jaffa in.'

I ran upstairs and hastily pulled on a pair of crumpled jeans I'd thrown on a chair the night before, found a half-clean T-shirt and pulled my hair back into a scrunchie, then I raced back down to stuff some toast in my mouth. Dad was cradling Jaffa in his arms, stroking her head and cooing to her. 'I'm sure I heard her purr just now,' he said, looking up at me as I clattered my plate into the sink and washed my hands. I ignored him. I was beginning to get a bit annoyed about his obsession with Jaffa talking. It was like when he'd suggested names for Jaffa: it made me feel left out somehow.

Dad didn't notice my lack of response. He was wittering on, looking lovingly at the kitten as he spoke. 'I was thinking about how we don't know her age. While you were lazing around in bed I did a bit of surfing on the internet to get advice on what to do if you find a stray kitten.'

'Jaffa's not a stray!' I protested, flinching at his comment about me 'lazing around' while he did research on *my* kitten. 'I was *given* her.'

'I know,' Dad said, soothingly. 'But Fenella didn't know how old she was, did she? She made out that her cat had found Jaffa.' He laughed. 'I know she's a bit bonkers, but she was quite clear that she didn't know where Jaffa had come from. And anyway, on this website I was looking at, it says that as well as getting Jaffa inoculated against all kinds of lurgies, we need to make sure we worm her regularly. And then there are fleas and ticks, of course.'

Dad handed me Jaffa and disappeared into the cupboard under the stairs in the hallway. He re-emerged with a cardboard box with a lid – it looked like a big shoe box. 'This will have to do; it had my new wellies in it,' he said, hastily puncturing some holes in the lid with a pair of scissors.

'What are you doing?' I asked in alarm.

'Making some air holes. Right. Put her in, keep the lid on and hold on tight. We don't want her getting out while I'm driving.'

I did as I was told, a scowl fixed firmly on my face. Then I checked the box lid was on tightly and followed Dad to the car.

Jaffa had looked so tiny when I put her in that cardboard box. She sat in the bottom staring up at me, her expression even more anxious than ever. I felt dreadful, like I was deceiving her, taking her to a place where a huge human was going to lean over her and stick needles in her.

'Don't worry, little Jaffa Cake,' I crooned nervously through the sides of the box. 'I'll take care of you. We're just going for a short drive. You hold on in there, now.' At that precise moment, I was secretly feeling relieved that Jaffa and I were *not* on the sort of speaking terms I'd been on with Kaboodle. If Jaffa had been able to pick up on the nerves in my voice, she would have sensed right away that something horrid was about to happen to her.

Dad opened the car door for me and I slid on to the back seat, clutching the box firmly to my chest. Then he reached across and strapped me in and I settled the box on my lap.

'What's up, Bertie?' he asked, scrutinizing me before putting his key in the ignition.

'Nothing,' I muttered sullenly.

'Are you worried about the vet?' he persisted.

I remained silent and stared out of the windscreen.

Dad bit his lip. 'I know it's not nice, Jaffa having injections, but you know it's for her own good, don't you?'

I felt my sulk begin to thaw around the edges. Poor Dad – it wasn't really his fault I was grumpy. I was just all mixed up about Jazz going off like that and Jaffa being so silent on me.

'It's just – you don't think she'll freak, being shut up in the dark in this box, do you?' I asked anxiously, glancing at Dad.

He'd reversed out of the drive now and was concentrating on turning out of our road, but he smiled and said, 'She'll be OK. It's not far to the vet's. She needs to be contained, though; I don't want her doing her James Bond act while I'm driving, shinning up the back of the seat and walking on the ceiling.'

I couldn't help letting slip a giggle at that image.

'Secret Agent Double-0 Supercat reporting for duty, sir!' Dad said, putting on a serious spy-type voice which made me giggle even more. 'Claws sharpened and ready for action!'

I glanced down at the box and wondered what

the little cat was thinking. 'What a pair of loonies,' probably.

Dad changed gear and sped up as we joined the main road. I felt a stab of alarm as Jaffa began sliding about inside the box, and I could hear her claws scrabbling desperately to try and get a hold on the cardboard.

'Dad! Dad! Slow down!' I cried, trying to steady her.

'What do you mean? I'm only going at about twenty miles an hour!' he protested. 'The way this traffic is going—'

'Well, it's too fast for Jaffa,' I told him. 'She's in a right state!'

'We might as well walk then,' he said impatiently.

I knew that wasn't an option: I wouldn't be able to keep Jaffa in the box if we walked. Reluctantly I held on even more firmly, glad for the second time that morning that the little cat couldn't tell me exactly what she thought of me.

We got to the vet's to find there was a huge crowd of people in the waiting room. At least the smaller animals were kept separate from the larger ones, I thought, as we were shepherded away from a room full of dogs of every colour, shape and size, all straining at their leashes and drooling and yapping at each other.

'Looks like you were right about the lid,' I said to Dad grudgingly.

'Mmm,' he nodded, eyeing the seething horde of dogs.

I cautiously placed the box down on a seat. Jaffa had been hurtling around in a frenzy during the journey, and now she was bashing the top of the box so hard, it felt like she was trying to headbutt her way out of there. I held on tighter than ever and sighed as I looked at the large group of people waiting to be seen with their cats, guinea pigs, rabbits, hamsters and – urgh! I shuddered as a sudden movement in a glass tank caught my eye. It was – it couldn't be, could it—?

'Oh my— Did you see that?' Dad whispered, horror consuming his features. He was staring at the glass tank too, his eyes boggling out of their sockets.

I gulped and nodded. 'A snake!' I mouthed.

Dad and I exchanged incredulous looks and then stared resolutely at the floor. Every time the receptionist called for someone to go in to the vet, I prayed hard that it would be the snake's turn so that I didn't have to sit there, knowing I was sharing a room with it. But it seemed it had arrived far too early for its appointment, as a stream of other animals were called in first. I sneaked a peek at it only to look away again quickly. It had reared its head up and stared right at me, its forked tongue quivering, as though sizing me up for its dinner. I shivered. Did snakes eat kittens? I pushed the horrifying thought away and clutched the box closer to my chest.

Pins and Needles

As I forced myself to look at the cuter animals in the waiting room, it suddenly struck me as odd that Jaffa had not uttered a single sound the whole time she'd been ricocheting around inside the box. I mean, you would have thought that being frightened and shut in like that might have wrenched at least a little mew out of her. Weird.

I watched the hands move round on the clock and felt my head nod forward sleepily.

'Jaffa Fletcher!'

Dad jabbed me in the ribs, jolting me wide awake.

'That's us,' he said out of the side of his mouth. 'How ridiculous, giving a kitten a surname!'

'She's part of the family now, Dad,' I teased, following him through the door.

The vet was waiting by a high table in the middle of a small ultra-white room which reminded me of the dentist's, except there wasn't one of those black leather chairs that look like something you'd see in an evil master criminal's torture chamber. There wasn't much in the room at all, actually. Apart from the table, there was just a very stern-looking skinny woman in a white coat and a veterinary nurse in a green uniform who was about five times the size of the vet and looked so muscly and tough that I thought at first she was a man until I realized her uniform was a dress. Behind this terrifying pair were lots and lots of white cupboards that all looked the same. How would you ever remember where you'd put things? I wondered.

'So this is – *Jaffa*?' the skinny woman asked, as if the name left a nasty taste in her mouth. She gestured towards the box and curled her lip.

I nodded. I was struck absolutely dumb. I was now in a *real* vet's surgery with Jaffa, my own *real* kitten!

'Let's take a look then, shall we?' the vet said, carefully lifting the lid.

Not carefully enough, as it happened.

'Aiiiiiee!' Dad yelled, as a streak of ginger and white shot out of the box like a firefly and went scooting round the tiny room, bouncing off the walls in an attempt to escape.

I squealed in fright as I thought someone would end up stepping on her, and backed myself into a corner while Dad hopped nervously from foot to foot telling me to 'do something'.

Luckily, neither the vet nor the nurse seemed at all fazed, and in a swift pincer movement they swooped down on poor confused Jaffa and caught her.

The vet lifted her up by the scruff of the neck in much the same way I had seen Kaboodle hold her just a few days ago.

'Not so fast, you little scamp,' she said sharply.

'Ca-can I ask a question?' I stammered. The woman was so scary, and all the white and the shining metal things everywhere made me distinctly nervous.

'Hmm?' the vet said impatiently, Jaffa still dangling in mid-air from her long rubber-glove-encased fingers like a specimen in a laboratory experiment.

'It's just – well, it might sound weird, and it might be totally normal but because I haven't had a kitten before I don't know, but—'

'And your point is?' the vet cut in. She was tapping her foot now, and the nurse was smirking at me.

'I – well, is it normal for a kitten not to mew?'

The vet snorted. 'Of course it's normal. This one's only a few weeks old. Probably ten or eleven. You should have brought her in before this, of course, so that she could have her first jabs. She's probably riddled with worms.' Dad shuddered. 'As for mewing, some kittens are very quiet at first, some are not. Her voice will develop sooner or later, and then you'll probably wish she'd never started, she'll make such a racket. Especially around dinner time.'

I had a feeling this vet was not what you might call a 'cat person'.

Still, it was a relief to hear that Jaffa probably just hadn't quite found her voice yet. It made me hopeful that she might one day communicate with me after all.

The vet set Jaffa down on the black surface of the table while Dad chatted about how we'd been given her as a leaving gift by a friend and how we knew nothing about kittens. I tuned out and let him do all the talking as I was feeling too intimidated by the spiky white vet with her laser-sharp tongue to offer any information myself.

I don't think the vet would have taken any notice of me anyway. She certainly didn't look as if she was listening to Dad. She had bent down so that she was at eye level with Jaffa and the pair were staring each other out. The vet kept her hand firmly on the back

73

of Jaffa's neck the whole time, but I didn't think she needed to: Jaffa's liquid eyes were fixed unblinkingly on the woman. I wondered if she was thinking the same thing I was: Jaffa the feline firework had met her match.

'That's better. I always win in the end, young lady,' the vet told Jaffa. 'Now we're just going to check you over, and then a quick injection and you'll be out of here.'

I'm sure her eyes glinted wickedly as she said 'injection'.

The vet held her hand out to the nurse, who placed in it a small black object which looked like a pocket torch. Then the vet swiftly touched each of Jaffa's ears with it.

'Ears fine,' she said. The nurse grunted and tapped something into the computer on the surface behind her.

The vet then tipped Jaffa's head back, so fast it seemed to take the kitten by surprise. Using her thumb and forefinger she squeezed Jaffa's mouth open and glanced at the rows of needle-sharp white teeth.

'Teeth fine,' she said. The nurse grunted again and tapped away. 'Syringe ready?' the vet asked her.

The nurse nodded and handed over a small metal tray with a syringe, the plunger pulled back and ready for action. I swallowed drily. The needle looked far too big for my tiny kitten. I wasn't sure I could watch.

The vet glanced at me sharply. 'No fainting in my surgery!' she said and pulled a grimace which I supposed was her attempt at a smile.

I looked at Dad for reassurance and put out my hand so he could hold it, but he appeared to be fixated on something behind the vet's back, and his face had gone a funny greyish colour.

'Dad?' I whispered.

Hiisssss!

Kitten Wars

My head swivelled at the unfamiliar noise.

There, on the top of the white cupboards, sliding noiselessly towards the nurse at the computer, was the snake!

I shrieked, one hand flying to my mouth, the other gesturing wildly at the scaly reptile. The vet had been about to insert the needle into a pinch of Jaffa's flesh, but she jumped when I screamed and the needle slipped and went into Jaffa far too quickly.

'Aaaaaooooooow!' The poor little kitten's eyes were bulging out of her face and she let out a strangled cry of pain and anguish. The vet held on to her firmly, all the colour draining from her as she followed my gaze.

As for me, it was as if the snake had hypnotized me and turned me to stone. My head was spinning with confusion: Jaffa had finally found her voice! *And*, what's more, there was a real live snake on the loose . . . Was any of this really happening?

Pins and Needles

The vet let the syringe drop, commanded me through gritted teeth to hold on to Jaffa and then darted forward in a terrifying kung-fu-style action. She grabbed the snake with lightning speed, one bony hand around its sinewy body, the other immobilizing its jaws. I half expected her to utter a piercing 'Haaaeeee-yah!' or maybe to chop the snake in two with her bare hands.

But she simply handed the snake to the nurse with terse instructions to go and find the owner, then calmly placed the syringe back on the tray and pulled off her white rubber gloves, saying, 'There, all done,' in a smug and satisfied tone.

Thank goodness for that, I thought, some sensation returning to my limbs. Now let's get out of this hellhole.

I turned to Dad to ask him to help me with Jaffa.

But he wasn't going to be much use to me.

He had fainted.

6

The Great Escape

We got out of there eventually, with Jaffa hissing and spitting and sticking her legs out in all directions to make it as difficult as possible to get her back into the box. The vet's reaction to Dad fainting was as brusque as her method of dealing with the snake: she threw a large mug of water in his face, gave him another mug of water to drink and told him to go and sit in the waiting room until he felt safe enough to drive.

'Blimey, she was a tough cookie, that one!' Dad said feebly when he at last felt strong enough to stagger to the reception area to pay the bill. 'Not cheap either,' he muttered, as he handed over his credit card with shaking fingers.

I held my breath, waiting for what I was sure would come next: *Not sure about this having-a-kitten lark* . . .

'Still, she's a sweetie, little Jaffs, isn't she?' Dad said, grinning weakly. 'Come on, let's go home. I don't know about you, but I need some food after all that excitement.'

I let out a whoosh of relief and grinned too.

'Will you keep an eye on Jaffa for the rest of the day?' Dad asked as we drove home (more slowly than we'd driven *to* the vet's, I noticed – Dad was clearly feeling more ropy than he was letting on).

'OK,' I said. 'I won't let her out of my sight.'

'Only you heard what the vet said as we left? I must admit I didn't quite catch all of it –' No, still recovering from your fainting fit! – 'but I'm pretty sure she said something about how cats go and hide after traumatic experiences, and I think it's fair to say this trip to the vet's counts as one xperience. I feel a bit like hiding myself!'

s all right,' I assured him. 'I'll take her up to my room. She can sleep on my bed.'

But, as with a lot of things in my life, it didn't turn out to be that simple.

When we got home, Dad set about cooking us some lunch.

I took Jaffa upstairs in the box and placed it on my bed. I carefully removed the lid and peered inside to see her looking at me with a definite note of reproach in her clear blue eyes. I could have sworn the corners of her mouth were turned down too, in a heartbreakingly sad expression.

'Oh, little Jaffa Cake!' I cooed, picking her up gently and holding her close to my chest. She felt stiff and unyielding as if she were solid with fright. 'I'm so sorry. It's been a horrible morning. But you're safe at home now.'

Jaffa relaxed a bit and I felt a slight vibration from

her body. I pushed my hands away from my chest slightly so that I could take a good look at her.

'Are you purring?' She inclined her head slightly. Oh my goodness! Maybe I was getting somewhere at last. 'Are you trying to talk to me, little one?'

The vibrations increased a fraction. It was definitely the beginnings of a purr, although there was still no sound from her mouth.

'Bertie!' Dad was yelling up the stairs. 'Can you come and lay the table, please?'

I rolled my eyes at Jaffa. 'Better do what the man says.'

The purring went up a notch further. And a whole field of butterflies took off in my stomach. Was Jaffa finding her voice?

I held her softly to me as I went downstairs to help Dad. 'Dad, you won't believe this, but Jaffs is purring!' I told him. 'Listen!'

Dad came over and stroked the top of her head with one finger, the wooden spoon he was mixing the sauce with in his other hand. 'Aw, that's adorable! Hey – before I forget, we ought to write the next vet's appointment down on the calendar.'

'What?' I started. *Another* appointment? I felt Jaffa tense in my arms.

'Yes, you heard what she said as we were leaving, didn't you? Honestly, Bertie, *I* was the one that fainted!' Dad ruffled my hair in that annoying way he had when he was teasing me.

I brushed his hand away irritably. 'She's not going back there,' I said firmly.

'She has to,' Dad insisted. 'That injection today was just the first. She has to have a couple of follow-up jabs in four weeks' time.'

Immediately Dad said this, Jaffa jabbed *me* – hard – with her pointy claws, leaped out of my arms and disappeared out of the kitchen, a blur of white and orange.

'Yow! Go after her, Dad!' I screamed, rubbing my arm.

The Great Escape

Dad swivelled his head back and forth, the spoon still in one hand. He looked like a crazy meerkat up on its hind legs staring manically with huge wide eyes. It would have been funny if I weren't in such a panic.

'Where's she gone?' Dad shouted. He darted out of the room into the hall and then sped around the house, checking in all the rooms under tables, chairs, wardrobes, beds.

I chased after him, shouting, 'This is your fault, Dad! You should never have mentioned the vet.'

Dad stopped in his tracks and glared at me. 'What are you on about?' he demanded. 'What's the vet got to do with this?'

I huffed dramatically. 'You know what a horrendous time she had this morning, and then you go and tell her she's got to go back there in four weeks' time!'

Dad put his hands on my shoulders and stared into my eyes. I was vaguely aware of the spoon dripping sauce down my back. 'Bertie,' he said slowly, 'Jaffa is a kitten. She can't understand us.'

Whoops! 'Y-y-yeah, I know that,' I faltered and looked shiftily away. 'It's just . . . why else would she shoot off like that the moment you mention the vet?' My voice was rising and I could feel my chest knotting in panic. I didn't want Dad to start suspecting anything about my attempts at cat-communication, but on the other hand, I had to get my point across. He couldn't go round saying things that might possibly upset Jaffa. 'Sh-she was quite happy and cosy in my arms until you said the word 'injection', that's all. You know what they say about cats and their sixth sense . . .' I tailed off before I dug myself in any deeper.

Luckily Dad seemed more concerned about me being upset than losing my marbles. 'She's prob-ably hiding in a corner somewhere,' he said calmly. 'After all, she is so small – she could get into the narrowest gap.'

The Great Escape

I nodded miserably. It wasn't as if Jaffa could get out of the house. I glanced into the utility room.

'Dad! Why is the back door open?' I shouted.

Dad whirled round and ran into the garden. 'Oh no!' he breathed. 'I opened it to get rid of the smell of onions. You don't think—?'

'Well, we haven't found her inside, have we?' I snarled. 'Thanks a bunch, Dad. You *know* we have to keep her in — she's too young to go roaming the streets,' I added, borrowing one of Dad's own favourite phrases.

He blanched. 'I'll go out now and see if I can find her. You stay here and watch the lunch and keep an eye out in case she's still in the house somewhere.'

'But—'

'Please, Bertie,' Dad said anxiously. 'She may still be in the house, and there's no point in the two of us wandering around out there.'

I could tell he felt really guilty. There was no point in me saying anything else. I would just have to sit tight and wait.

But of course I didn't just sit there — I scoured the house from top to bottom. I stood in the bathroom, staring at the ceiling and thinking maybe I should go up into the loft, although I knew that was a fruit-loop idea, as how could a kitten open the latch, get the ladder down and close the latch behind her? But then I'd known stranger things, such as escaping hamsters. And snakes.

I shuddered.

I couldn't bear the thought of Jaffa out there somewhere, lost and scared and all alone. What if she'd run out into someone's garden and got herself locked in a shed or a garage? What if it was dark and cobwebby? What if she'd been chased by a dog? She'd had enough frights for one day. So had I. I kicked the side of the shower in frustration and then jumped as a high-pitched screaming noise started up in the kitchen.

'The smoke alarm!'

The Great Escape

I raced back down the stairs.

It was our lunch. I'd left it stewing away, and the sauce had boiled down and become a dark solidifying gluey mess.

Not that I cared. I wasn't hungry. Where was Dad? When was he coming back? Would he come back with Jaffa?

I suddenly felt very small and alone. It crossed my mind that if I still had a mum, she would have stayed with me while Dad went out looking for Jaffa. She would have given me a cuddle and kept me calm. And the lunch would not have been ruined.

A sob rippled through me as I went to fetch a mop and poked the handle end at the smoke alarm to switch it off, then opened the windows to let the smoke out. No point in keeping the house closed up any more. Jaffa wasn't there, I knew. I put the pans to soak in the sink and flopped down on the sofa in the sitting room and waited, tears streaming down my face.

'Jazz!' I said out loud. I should call her and tell her what had happened, then she could keep an eye out for Jaffa too. But then I remembered what she'd said about me being obsessed with the kitten and not interested in anything else.

Still, it was worth a shot, wasn't it? She was my best friend after all, and she might just be able to help. Especially if she knew how upset I was.

I picked up the house phone and dialled her number, praying she'd be in. Praying that she'd want to talk to me.

I'd just pressed the last number when the front door opened.

'Dad!' I put the phone down. He was carrying a bundle of something and looking very hot and bothered and he had streaks of dirt down the front of his T-shirt.

'H-have you got her?' I stammered.

'Yes,' Dad said, looking sheepish. 'She was hiding under a car over the road, outside number 15! I went all round the close, and then I saw something flashing under the car as I came round the corner – a pair of bright blue eyes, as it happened. Thank goodness she's OK.'

'How on earth did you get her out from under the car?' I asked.

'By sliding under it and talking to her and reassuring her,' he said, flushing a deep red. What? I was glad I hadn't been out there in the street with him. What if someone had seen him? 'I'm beginning to think you might be right about her understanding every word we say,' Dad added.

My heart bounced into my mouth and did a backflip. 'Really?'

'I don't mean literally,' he laughed shakily, 'but put it this way: when I spoke to her in a calm voice and told her everything would be OK and that I was really, really sorry and wouldn't let her see that bossy old bat at the vet's again, she came slinking towards me and let me pick her up.'

'But – well, is that true? About not going back? What about the injec—?'

'Don't!' Dad said. And then he lowered his voice until he was all but mouthing the words: 'We'll talk about it later.'

I nodded, feeling slightly daft that we were whispering in front of a cat. I held out my arms to Jaffa and Dad put her gently in the palms of my hands and hugged me to him. Good old Dad.

'Welcome home, little sweetheart,' I breathed. 'Don't you go running off again, OK?'

Jaffa blinked at me and nuzzled my hand with her fluffy head and I felt that heart-racing vibration again. That faint, kitten-style purr.

Everything was going to be all right. Wasn't it?

7

Hot Gossip

Ever since the Great Escape, I had been on constant alert, walking around the place like a cat on hot coals in case Jaffa tried to do a runner again. And Dad wasn't much help because he was really busy with meetings about his latest play.

'Why don't you call Jazz and at least ask her to come round?' he said. 'She could help you keep an eye on Jaffs and it would be company for you.'

But I couldn't quite face speaking to Jazz just then. She hadn't exactly tried to get hold of *me* since our last conversation (if that's what you'd call it). Besides, I had Jaffa; I wasn't lonely.

'It's OK, Dad,' I tried to reassure him. 'I've got

my hands full with this bouncy kitten! I promise not to open the door or answer the house phone while you're out. I'm nearly twelve, for goodness sake!'

When I had Jaffa in my sights and wasn't worried about her running off, it was fun hunkering down with my kitten with no one else to distract us. I made her some toys from bits of string and paper and spent hours dragging them across the floor and giggling every time she pounced on them. She always looked so proud of her-self when she 'caught' one.

She was so cute the way she practised fighting and hunting with shad-ows, bees and flies. And there was nothing snug-glier than curling up in front of the telly with that bundle of fluff on my lap.

But I had to admit, apart from her purr, which was getting louder by the day, Jaffa did not seem to want to (or be able to) talk to me.

'Come on, little Jaffsie,' I coaxed. 'Tell Bertie what you're thinking, eh?' I tickled her under her white chin.

Her purrs increased in volume and she closed her eyes ecstatically, her mouth turned up in what I was sure was a Cheshire Cat grin.

'You like that, don't you?' I tried again.

Her smile widened and she opened one eye.

I stopped tickling and Jaffa immediately opened both eyes and sat up straight. She put her head on one side and let out a whining mew.

'Oh, so you don't want me to stop tickling?' I asked.

She blinked and rubbed her head against my hand. This was beginning to feel like a conversation! My heart skipped a beat.

'So? Shall I do it some more?' I pressed on. But apart from purring louder than ever, she didn't say a word.

93

★

After two days of this, I had to admit that I was getting bored and was in desperate need of some human company.

So on the third morning, when Dad announced he would be at home, I swallowed my pride and decided to go and see Jazz. What was the worst that could happen? I aked myself, ignoring the nerves that were fizzing around inside me.

'Dad, I'm going round to Jazz's, OK?' I peered round the door to his office. Dad was staring at his laptop as if it possessed the key to the secrets of the universe.

'Mmm?' he said, blinking at me like a dormouse coming out of hibernation.

'You all right?' I asked. I narrowed my eyes. He looked even more dopey than usual. I hoped he wasn't getting ill. The last time Dad was ill, he went to bed and pulled the duvet over his head and I thought he was going to die. Turned out to be a cold, but you would have thought he needed open-heart surgery the way he carried on. Jazz's mum says it's called Man Flu – Jazz's dad gets it every winter, apparently.

'Me?' Dad asked, blinking again. 'Yeah, I'm – I've got a bit stuck on the next scene, that's all. All those meetings have disrupted my schedule and I've literally lost the plot – hahaha! Er, what did you say about Jazz just then?'

I rolled my eyes at his bad pun. 'I *said* I'm going round there, OK? We – er – we need to talk.'

Dad shook his head. 'If you say so. Where's Jaffa?' he added distractedly.

'I just checked: she's asleep on my bed. I've shut her in there and put a litter tray by the door so you don't have to bother with her till I get back. I'll be home for tea,' I added.

Dad nodded. He was staring at the screen again. I doubted he'd listened to a word I'd said.

As I walked round the corner to Jazz's house, I

felt more and more anxious about seeing her again. For the first time in the whole of our friendship, I didn't really know what I was going to say to her, but I made myself keep putting one foot in front of the other all the way to her house.

I took a deep breath and rang the doorbell before I could change my mind and leg it back home.

The door was flung open so fast I gasped and stepped back.

'JA-AZZ! It's Bertie − you know, the one you were getting all stressy about,' shouted Ty, Jazz's younger brother.

What did *that* mean?

Jazz hurtled down the stairs and pushed her brother out of the way. This did not look good. Maybe I should have called first after all. Maybe she wouldn't want to see me, especially if she was so 'stressy' about me that she had told her family about it.

In one swift gesture, Jazz confirmed all my suspicions: she crossed her arms tightly and stood with one hip sticking out, her lips pursed, creating what can only be described as her seriously–not–amused pose.

'Hi!' I said. Bit pathetic, but what else was I supposed to say?

'What?' she said.

'Er . . . hi,' I repeated.

'Right, is that all? Only I'm kind of busy right now.'

My stomach squeezed in on itself. I dug my fingernails into the palms of my hands to keep a hold on things.

'Oh,' I said. Great. It seemed I had lost the power of speech.

'Okaaay,' Jazz said slowly, looking somewhere over my shoulder as if I was becoming invisible. 'I'm going to close the door then. It's getting draughty.'

'Jazz, look! Huckleberry's climbing up my

97

tummy — whoo. It tickles!' Ty had re-emerged and there was something crazy going on inside his sweatshirt. It was jumping and wriggling and, wait, was it *squeaking* too?

Jazz whirled round and let rip at her brother. 'Tyson Brown, I'm going to KILL you! Come here!'

But too late — Ty and the wriggling sweatshirt were off down the hall at full pelt, Jazz screeching after him like a hawk on the attack.

The door was still open, so I thought I might as well go into the house. I was pretty intrigued about what Ty had done that was making Jazz so mad. And I couldn't help feeling grateful to him for distracting his sister from giving me the cold shoulder.

The shrieking and yelling from the kitchen brought Jazz's big sister, Aleisha, tearing downstairs.

'What on earth—? Oh, hi Bertie.' She stopped when she caught sight of me and smiled. 'Good to see you – you and Jazz made up then?'

Made up? So Jazz *had* told her whole family we'd had a fight? I must have looked shocked, because Aleisha blushed and stammered, 'Oh, right, none of my business. But hey, I'd better go and see what the brats are brawling about now. You coming?'

I wasn't sure I wanted to now: the noise from the kitchen had reached a new level of hysteria, and added to Jazz's yelling and Ty's protestations there was a shriller, more distressed squeaking.

'Break it up, you two!' Aleisha shouted above the commotion, waving her hands in the air like a referee at a football match. And then: 'Oh my— Ty, put Huckleberry down NOW!'

The noise from Jazz and her little brother ceased immediately, and Tyson dropped what he had been wrestling from Jazz's grasp.

I screamed. A brown furry thing the size of my shoe ran past me and zipped under the dresser, squeaking furiously as it went.

'Upstairs!' Aleisha barked at her brother. 'And you had better coax the poor thing out from under there,' she told Jazz. 'You'll be lucky if it doesn't have a heart attack after what you two have just put it through.'

'He's a HE, not an *it*,' said Ty sullenly, but catching the steely look in his older sister's eyes, he ran out of the room.

Jazz was already on her knees looking under the dresser and muttering something about new trainers getting dirty.

Aleisha raised one eyebrow at me and said, 'Good luck,' and then swept out of the room after Ty.

Jazz was reaching her arm as far as she could under the dresser and calling out in a high-pitched voice, 'Come on out, Huckleberry. Come on, cutie-pie. I'm sorry. The nasty boy's gone now.'

I shuffled from foot to foot. I had obviously picked a really bad time to come round, but I was pretty hacked off that Jazz wasn't explaining who or what Huckleberry was. It was obvious he was some kind of animal, but Jazz didn't have any pets. So why was she suddenly looking after one and why hadn't she told me?

'Jazz – who is Huckleberry?' I asked loudly, getting down on my knees beside her.

She frowned up at me, her arm still stretched out underneath the dresser, moving from side to side. 'As if you care,' she snapped.

'Of course I care!' I protested, irritation rising up inside me. I sat up and slumped back on to my heels. 'Jazz,' I said trying to keep my feelings under control, 'I've obviously done something to really upset you, but believe me, if I knew what it was I'd sort it out—'

Jazz rolled her eyes. 'Well, if you don't know what it is, *I* can't help you.'

She sounded like one of our teachers. I snapped. 'Listen, Jazz, if you're going to get all high and mighty with me, forget it. I was going to offer to help you with whatever you're doing down here, cos after what Aleisha said about heart attacks it sounded serious. But you know what? I think I'll just go home and leave you to it.'

I pushed myself up and dusted my jeans down, giving Jazz time to apologize. She didn't, so I walked out of the room.

I was heading for the front door, steam coming out of my ears, when I heard her shout, 'I'm sorry! I'm sorry! Come back, Bert. Please?'

I turned round to see a dusty, dishevelled Jazz standing in the doorway to the kitchen, cradling a dusty and dishevelled lump of brown fur in her arms.

Curiosity welled up enough to quash my annoyance, so I walked towards her. It wasn't until I was up really close that I saw what it was that Jazz was holding.

'Say hi to Huckleberry,' she said, smiling faintly.

My stony heart melted.

'Oh my goodness! What a gorgeous little thing!' I raced over and held out my hands. 'Can I have a cuddle?'

Jazz handed the creature over (a little quickly, I noticed). 'Sure,' she said.

Huckleberry had started up a huge racket the minute he was put into my arms, squirming around, squeaking and trying to nibble my sleeve. I giggled. 'He's a wriggler, isn't he?'

'Oh yeah,' said Jazz with feeling. 'It turns out guinea pigs are not the nice quiet easy pets I thought they were going to be. Rats with attitude, if you ask me.' (I chewed my lip to stop myself from smirking: not so long ago, when I first set up my Pet-Sitting Service, Jazz had said she hoped we would get to look after guinea pigs because she 'luuurrved' them.) 'Also turns out my brother has the attention span of the average fruit fly and has already given up on Huckleberry, so it's down to Guess Who to look after him.'

'Oh, right. So he's *Ty's* pet? That makes sense.'

Jazz frowned at me. 'What's that supposed to mean?'

'N–nothing!' I stammered. 'I just meant – well, I was thinking that you didn't exactly seem enthusiastic about Huckleberry?' I stopped. I was in danger of digging a hole too deep to get out of.

Jazz had the beginnings of a mad-bad-and-dangerous-to-know look on her face. But then the cloud passed and she let out a long slow breath and said, 'Yeah, which is why me becoming Huckleberry's Next Best Owner is not really my idea of fun. It's cool you're here actually, Bertie. You can give me some advice.'

I felt my shoulders relax. Everything was going to be all right. Jazz and I were still friends.

We went into the TV room. Huckleberry's cage was on a table by the window, so I carefully un-hooked his little claws from my jumper and placed him gently inside. I couldn't help feeling a bit envious. This little guy was a barrel of fun and his cage was awesome: full of tubes for him to scurry in and out of, piles of sawdust and a little cubby hole for him to sleep in. It looked like one of the ones I'd seen in Paws for Thought. Shame Ty and Jazz didn't seem to appreciate the little guy.

'Did you get him from that lady round the corner?' I asked. 'The one you told me about when I had the Pet-Sitting Service?'

Jazz flopped down on to a beanbag and I slumped down next to her. 'Telly?' she asked, reaching for the remote and completely ignoring my question. 'I've got this cool new DVD from the last series of *Who's Got Talent?* It's this behind-the-stage thing? They show you all the interviews with the guys who got into the finals. I sooooo wish I could audition for the next one!' she babbled.

'Right,' I said, disappointed. What had happened to asking me for advice about Huckleberry? But I guessed I was lucky Jazz wanted to spend time with me at all, the way things had been lately, even if I was going to have to sit through this rubbish.

We snuggled down and Jazz fiddled about with the remote. The screen blazed with light and noise and I groaned inwardly as a bunch of people with weird clothes and horrible hair started screaming and whooping and yelling about how being on *Who's Got Talent?* was their 'dream come true' and it had been 'just the most incredible journey' and how it had 'changed their lives forever'. Jazz was whooping and yelling in agreement and seemed to have completely forgotten that I was there.

I was just thinking that maybe I should slip away quietly and get back to Jaffa, when Jazz's mum came into the room.

'Hi, Bertie! Haven't seen you for a while. You OK?'

I nodded. 'Yes, thanks.'

'Great!' She smiled her huge, glossy smile which always made a warm feeling spread like sunshine inside me. 'Want to hear some interesting news?'

Jazz frowned. 'Shh!' she snapped.

Jazz's mum went over to the TV and turned it off, silencing her daughter's protests with a don't-start-with-me-young-lady look in her big brown eyes. 'You shouldn't be watching telly on a lovely day like this!'

'B-but—!' Jazz started.

'Jazz,' Mrs B said, a dangerous note of warning creeping into her voice. Then she looked at me and grinned apologetically. 'So, as I was saying. You know those new neighbours?'

Jazz crossed her arms and flicked her head back stroppily. 'What about them?' she said, trying to sound like she didn't give a stuff.

But her eyes were shining. I focused on not smirking. Jazz couldn't wait to meet that boy she'd told me about. It was so obvious.

Mrs Brown immediately drew herself up to her full height, squaring up to her daughter. It was always a pretty impressive sight when Jazz and her mum had a face-off. I quite enjoyed being a spectator, but deep down was relieved I was not involved. Put it this way: when Jazz's mum was putting on her tough act, I could see where her youngest daughter got it from.

'I thought Bertie would like to know – seeing as she's going to be living opposite these people,' Mrs Brown began tartly, 'that Mr Smythe told me—'

'Mr Smythe! Whoo! Hamster Man!' Jazz crowed, putting her hands up to her face as if she were nibbling a carrot and twitching her nose in a realistic impression of a giant hamster.

'Ja-azz!' I protested, embarrassed at her impersonation. It was true, Mr Smythe did act as rodenty as his hamsters, Houdini and Mr Nibbles, but even so it was mortifying seeing Jazz take the mickey out of him in front of her mum.

'Sor-reeeee!' Jazz drawled, wobbling her head at me.

Hot Gossip

Mrs Brown sucked her teeth. 'OK, OK, I know he's a bit strange. But he's always been friendly to me. And anyway, he gave me some good advice about looking after guinea pigs,' she said, looking at me. 'Heaven knows no one in *this* household seems to be taking an interest.' She glared at Jazz. 'Anyway, I'm getting off the point. Mr Smythe says that the removal vans may arrive tonight, ahead of the family. You should probably tell your dad, Bertie. Oh yes, and he said these people may only be here for a short time – they're renting Fenella's place. She's not going to sell her house in case she wants to come back.'

My heart fluttered like a trapped moth at the words 'come back'. Did this mean I might see Kaboodle again soon? I would love to be able to ask him more questions about Jaffa. Where had she really come from? How come I couldn't seem to understand her? How could I get her to calm down and be less skittish around me? But my excitement faded at Mrs Brown's next words.

' – but it seems that's not going to be any time soon. Her career's really taken off since your dad wrote that play for her, Bertie, and she's been offered loads of work. Apparently she's got to travel a lot, so she's decided to let out her house for at least six months while she makes up her mind what to do—'

'Yeah, yeah. Tell us something we actually *want* to know,' Jazz butted in rudely.

Mrs Brown frowned and Jazz muttered another barely audible 'sor-reee' at the floor.

'Mr Smythe also told me some gossip about Fergus. But . . . I'm obviously intruding on your valuable time,' Jazz's mum teased, noting the sudden spark of interest on her daughter's face. 'I'll leave you girls to it.'

'But, Mum—' Jazz cried.

Mrs Brown turned her back on Jazz's frustrated bleating.

Hot Gossip

Jazz made to follow her, but Aleisha stuck her head around the door. 'What's up with you guys?' she asked. 'You look as if the world's about to end. Hey, did Mum tell you about the new boy? You know he's in a band, right? Well, you won't believe it – they've got an album deal already! How cool is that? I checked him out on the net.' She paused for effect and then said, 'He's lush!'

I felt my face collapse as Jazz started jumping up and down on the spot, squealing and squeaking like a hundred Huckleberries.

8
Moving In

At tea that night I asked Dad if he'd heard from Pinkella.

'Er . . . oh, yes,' he said vaguely, spooning baked beans into his mouth and staring into the middle distance. 'Why?'

'Just wondered if she'd told you anything about her tenants,' I said, trying to keep my voice light.

Dad blushed. 'Oh, sorry, Bertie, I should have told you – yes, there's a family coming to live in her house. They were supposed to arrive tonight, actually—'

'Yeah, I knew all that. But it's their *furniture* that's arriving tonight, actually. Jazz's mum told me,' I said pointedly. I felt a bit mean making Dad feel bad on purpose, but at the same time I wanted him to know I was fed up that I'd heard all the gossip from someone else.

'I've been distracted recently, haven't I?' Dad stammered, putting his cutlery down. 'It's just this new play I'm working on. And then all that hassle with Jaffa . . .'

'It's all right, really. The pressures of success, eh?' I laughed half-heartedly. I was happy that Dad was doing well and not having to work for the *Daily Ranter* any more. It meant he wasn't as grumpy as he used to be. But one thing that had not changed was the number of hours he worked. If anything he seemed to be working even harder than he had before. He was such a perfectionist. I remembered what Kaboodle had said about Dad doing it all for me. I did wish he would just stop sometimes, though.

It was all right for Jazz. If she was upset or excited

113

about something she could always talk to her mum or dad or Aleisha. Even having Ty around had to be better than being on your own.

'So, do you think we should invite them round?' Dad said, cutting into my gloomy thoughts. He was grinning widely and cheesily.

'Who?' I asked.

'The new neighbours.'

'NO WAY!'

'Hey, there's no need for that!' Dad frowned. 'What's the problem with being friendly?'

I shifted uncomfortably. 'I just don't really want to make a big deal out of them being our new neighbours, that's all.' I squirmed, remembering Jazz's excitement on learning how cool and good-looking the boy was meant to be.

Dad tutted. 'Don't worry. I won't embarrass you by wearing brightly coloured clothes or telling bad jokes or dying my hair green or anything,' he said sarcastically. 'Maybe I'll just go round there on my own and say "hi" once they've had a chance to settle in. I don't know — I hadn't even given it a moment's thought till now, to be honest . . . Right,' he said decisively, pushing back his chair. 'You done with that?' He gestured to my half-finished tea. I nodded. 'OK, well, I'm not going to do any more work tonight. How about a DVD?'

'Nah,' I said. 'I'm a bit tired. I'm going up to read. Might have an early night.' Truth was, I just wanted some time alone with Jaffa all snuggly on my bed.

But the little kitten had other ideas. She wouldn't settle at all and was off out of the room exploring before I could stop her. I did wonder if I should have followed her to make sure she was safe, but I knew all the doors and windows would be shut at this time. Anyway, as I passed my bedroom window I was distracted by a removal van pulling up opposite outside Pinkella's house.

It was quite late for them to be moving in, I

thought. I watched and waited to see what kind of stuff they would unload from the van, but no one came out. No sign of the family either.

I padded downstairs to tell Dad. He was half asleep in front of the TV, the newspaper open on his lap with Jaffa curled up on top of it and the remote in one hand.

'Dad?' I said softly.

'Wha—?' His head jerked up and he dropped the remote and jolted Jaffa awake. She shot into the air as if someone had plugged her tail into an electric socket and leaped on to the window sill. Dad shook his head and rubbed his eyes. 'Bertie, I thought you were in bed.'

'Yeah well, the removal van made a load of noise opposite.'

Dad glanced at the window. 'Oh, so they're here.'

I noticed Jaffa was watching the van intently, as if she expected someone she knew to come

out of it. I wondered if she
was thinking about
Kaboodle as I had
done earlier. 'Bit weird
to arrive so late, isn't it?' I
said, bringing myself out of dream-
land and into the present.

Dad shrugged. 'We don't know where they've
come from, do we? Sometimes these guys come
the night before they're going to do the removal –
means they can start first thing in the morning. They
can sleep in these vans, you know. Some of them
are kitted out with beds and stoves and stuff.'

Jaffa was sitting back on her haunches and patting
her paws against the window. It looked as though
she was trying to wave at the van.

I wonder if she thinks that's Kaboodle come
back, I thought. I certainly wished it was.

I didn't really know why the thought of this new
family was doing my head in so much. It was a bit

unfair of me, I knew that: I hadn't even caught a glimpse of them yet. But I had this nagging feeling that things were going to change as soon as they arrived. And something told me it wouldn't be for the better.

I scooped Jaffa up and gave Dad a kiss.

'Come on, Jaffs,' I mumbled into her cute triangle of an ear. 'Big day tomorrow, I guess. Let's get some sleep.'

I had no idea just how big a day it would turn out to be.

I was still snoozing when Dad hammered on my door the next morning. I peered bleary-eyed at my alarm clock. Only eight o'clock! In the holidays! What was so important he had to wake me up at *that* time for?

I stumbled out of bed and staggered to the door. Dad was standing on the other side of it, looking very sorry for himself. My first thought was he was cringing because I was looking a right muppet. I always did in the mornings. It was mostly the fault of my hair which had a life of its own that did not involve asking me for permission before restyling itself into a look that would probably best be described as Bomb-site of the Year.

But then as I rubbed my eyes and heard him say, 'Now I don't want you to worry, Bertie . . .' I realized that he was looking sheepish rather than cringing. Suddenly I was wide awake, my skin tingling in alarm.

'It's Jaffa, isn't it?' I cried.

'The thing is, I was putting the bins out and—'

DRIIING!

'The doorbell!' I yelled, rather unnecessarily. 'Go and get it, Dad – maybe someone's got her!'

'Don't panic, Bertie,' Dad said, sounding pretty unconvincing, I have to say. 'You get dressed and I'll answer the door.'

I muttered an ungracious 'Thanks' and ran back

into my room to scrabble around for some clothes. Stepping out of my PJs, I left them where they fell and hastily pulled on some pants and a half-clean top. I was just zipping up my jeans when there was the sound of bouncy footsteps on the stairs and Jazz appeared in the doorway.

'Boy, you look rough!' she said cheerily.

'Thanks so much.'

'Bertie!' It was Dad, yelling up the stairs. 'I'm going out to look for Jaffa!'

I glanced wildly at Jazz and then past her at the landing. I wanted to go with him, but Jazz was wearing her I'm-on-a-mission expression.

'So, can I look out your window?' she asked, pushing past me without waiting for an answer.

'Erm, well, no you can't. I'm kind of busy,' I said, anxious to get rid of her so I could chase after Jaffa.

'Hey, no need to be weird!' Jazz responded, curling her lip at me. She always curls her lip at me when she doesn't get something I've said. 'You've only just got up – you're not *busy* at all.'

'I am *about* to be busy,' I said stupidly. 'And anyway, I am not the one being weird. Seriously,' I added.

After all, she was the one who had just turned up at a time of the morning usually reserved for the kind of deranged people who say things like, 'We don't want to miss the best of the day now, do we?' (Yes we do. We want to sleep.) And as if that wasn't *weird* enough, she was now obsessed with looking out of my window. What's not to be freaked about?

Jazz shook her head impatiently. 'OK, OK, I know it's kind of early but I don't have anything to do today,' she said eventually, by way of an explanation. 'So.'

'So . . . ?' I said.

'So . . .' Jazz faltered, looking away for a second. 'I – er – I was thinking it might be fun to watch the new family move in. And you've got a better view from your place than I have from mine.' She fixed me with her deep brown eyes, challenging me to tell her I had other plans.

So *that* was what this was all about. I sighed.

'Oh come on, Bert,' Jazz wheedled, head on one side, her eyes growing huger by the minute. 'Aren't you even just a teensy bit curious to see what they're like?'

'Yeah, OK,' I admitted. 'Sorry, Jazz. It's just . . .' I decided to be honest in the hope that I'd at least be able to get out and leave Jazz curtain-twitching on her own. 'I'm really worried about Jaffa. She's just escaped again and she's still so young, and she's not really allowed out for another week cos she's only just had her vaccinations—'

'Oh, cats are always running off,' Jazz cut in, more than a hint of boredom creeping into her voice. 'You were the one who told me that, remember? When Kaboodle wasn't there that time and you thought he was dead and you ended up doing that memorial thing.' *ME?* It'd all been Jazz's idea as far as I was concerned. I raised my eyebrows, and she flushed as if reading my mind and then shook her head carelessly. 'Anyway, she's bound to want to come and go – it's what cats do, isn't it? So, can we look out of your window? The lorry's been there all night. And I saw the mum and dad carrying some boxes in from their car as I walked along the road just now. I tried to catch their eye, but they didn't spot me. Haven't seen the boy yet!' she added, her velvet eyes flashing with excitement.

Give me strength!

'OK, yeah. I'll just grab some binoculars, shall I?' I said sarcastically.

'Cool! Then we'll really be able to . . . Oh, you were joking,' she said, catching the look on my face.

Although binoculars wouldn't be such a bad idea, now I came to think of it. I could have used them

123

to see if Jaffa was out in the street somewhere.

'There!' Jazz squealed, wrenching me away from my mopey thoughts. She was pointing out of my window and jumping up and down.

'Where?' I shouted, thinking she'd seen Jaffa.

'Can you see him? Can you?' she cried.

My heart plummeted down to my bare feet as I realized she was pointing at the boy over the road. I tried to get a look at him, but Jazz was hogging the window, pressing her face up against it and breathing steam on the glass.

I stepped away and stared at my friend. Not only was her behaviour decidedly loopy this morning, she was looking pretty dressed up considering she'd only come round to hang out with me. Her hair had even more beads in it than usual and they made a right racket while she bounced around the place. She was wearing a denim miniskirt, purple leggings, purple and silver pumps and a purple T-shirt with a picture of a guitar on it in silver glitter and the word

'LOVE' in huge swirly letters.

'Bertie!' Jazz said, jabbing me in the arm with a very sharp finger. I glanced down, frowning – that had hurt!

'Are those *false nails?*' I asked her, my jaw dropping in total disbelief. What had got into her?

'Bertie, you are not listening to me,' Jazz said, ignoring my question and frowning. 'I asked you if you'd seen Fergus. You're not going to see much if you just stand there gawping at me like that.'

I chewed back a comment along the lines of 'You're the one who's gawping', and said sweetly, 'Sorry, Jazz. Just got a bit sidetracked by those talons of yours. And by the way, they're quite sharp, you know?' I rubbed my arm for dramatic effect.

Jazz's face darkened. 'Sor-ree. I think they're cool. Anyway, I don't want to talk about the finer arts of manicure,' she sneered. 'Come here and watch what's going on outside.'

I shuffled into the tiny space she had left me and

squashed up against the window. All I could see was the huge removal lorry (which I'd already seen quite enough of since it arrived last night), several men hoisting beds and garden furniture down a ramp and into the house, and a man and a woman standing by the front door pointing and gesturing.

'That's Fiona and Gavin Meerley,' Jazz said knowledgeably. 'The mum and dad— oh wow!' she interrupted herself. 'He's got a drum kit!' She rapped an excited rhythm on the pane with the freaky fingernails. 'And – do you reckon that's his guitar?' She pointed to a strange elongated parcel covered in thick brown paper. By the level of interest this had generated in my friend, I was pretty sure 'he' referred to this Fergus guy, not his dad.

'Hmm,' I said. I was scanning the contents of the lorry, which were coming out in quick succession. I wondered idly if these new people had any pets. Would I be able to guess from the stuff they had brought with them? Did you even pack pet stuff in a van when you moved?

'There! There!' Jazz shrieked again, breaking into my thoughts. I spotted a lanky figure slope out of the house, his hands in the pockets of his hugely baggy jeans, his longish hair flopping in his eyes. He mooched off around the side of the van and stood there for a moment, looking up and down the street. Jazz squealed again and jabbed noisily at the windowpane with her false nails.

And that's when Slouch Boy decided to look up and see my best mate doing her I'm-about-as-bonkers-as-it-gets routine in my bedroom window. I quickly shot out of sight, but not before I saw the boy smile sheepishly in our direction and wave. It was a smile which totally transformed his face from pretty normal-looking to mega-friendly-looking in an instant. I felt heat rush to my face and turned on Jazz.

'Now look what you've done!' I hissed.

'What do you mean?' Jazz retorted. 'It's not *my* fault! If you hadn't been so dopey in the first place

133

I wouldn't have had to point him out to you and then I wouldn't have tapped the window by mistake and then he wouldn't have looked up.' She paused to gaze dreamily out of the window. 'He's soooo *cool*!'

I snorted. 'Oh, you think so?'

Jazz flipped round. 'Yes. I do actually,' she spat. 'Why are you smirking?' she went on in a low voice. 'You're jealous, aren't you? I knew it!' she howled, throwing her hands up in the air.

'Oh, cut it out,' I said irritably. 'I don't even care who this loser is. I've had enough. I'm going to look for Jaffa.'

'*I'm going to look for Jaffa*,' Jazz mimicked in a sing-song voice.

'Yes, I am!' I butted in before she could say anything about what a baby I was thinking about my kitten all the time. 'And you know why? Because I care about her and I'm worried about her and I don't give a monkey's about a new family or a "lush" boy or anything else at the moment, actually. She's a tiny little cat out there all alone! Anything could happen!'

'Oh get a grip, Bertie!' Jazz muttered, rolling her eyes.

I gasped. What was happening between me and my best friend? She had never been so mean or un-interested in me before.

I burst into tears and stormed out of the room, down the stairs and out of the back door. I was about to slam the door with a final dramatic gesture when I remembered that I needed to take some keys with me. I whirled back into the utility room to grab them off the hook and came face to face with a very superior-looking Jazz.

'Honestly, all this fuss over a kitten. You do know you're overreacting, don't you?' she said pityingly. She shook her head as though I was a hopeless case. 'I guess I'll see you later.'

Then waving her ridiculous long nails at me, she sashayed out of my house and back into her own much more grown-up and sophisticated life.

9

Who's Got Talent?

We didn't find Jaffa. After we'd scoured the street, Dad said he'd go back and search every corner of the house just in case she had got back in somehow. Bit unlikely, I know, but we were feeling pretty desperate.

In the end I had to admit defeat. I was hot, thirsty and hungry. I hadn't had any breakfast, I remembered. I dragged my feet back home and made us some food.

'You could always put a poster up in the street,' Dad suggested through a mouthful of cheese sandwich. 'Or leave a plate of something really tasty out by the back door,' he added thoughtfully. 'And you know what? I think I'll go and get a cat flap today. Maybe she's been trying to get back in and hasn't been able to. What's her favourite food, d'you think?'

'She loves tuna,' I said feebly. 'Well, she loves the tuna-flavoured kitten food we got from Paws for Thought. Maybe we could try leaving some real tuna out?'

Dad rolled his eyes. 'OK. But don't be surprised if you have half the cats in town crowding round the back door.'

Even I managed a weak laugh at that. I could just imagine what Kaboodle would say. 'Fancy leaving tuna out for all the rabble to come and help themselves! Honestly, Bertie, you have no idea how we cats think . . .'

So Dad went out to buy a cat flap (and have a good natter with 'Bex' as well, no doubt!) and I fetched a tin of tuna and set it down outside the back door.

★

My mobile rang early the next day. Jazz had reprogrammed the ringtone again. It had made me laugh when she'd done it, but the way I was feel-ing right now, it wasn't doing anything to lighten my mood.

'You've got to come here – I've got so much to tell you. And show you!' Jazz announced breathily, hardly giving me enough time to say 'Hi'. 'He came round last night!' I grimaced quietly to myself. I didn't have to ask who 'he' was. And no sign of an apology from Jazz.

Still, I swallowed my sadness and told Dad I was going to Jazz's.

'We'll continue the search for Jaffa,' I said,

hoping against hope.

But of course, Jazz had very different plans.

'Quick, come upstairs – I don't want Ty to hear us talking,' she hissed, whisking me through the door so fast I nearly fell over my own feet. 'He was a right pain yesterday, shoving Huckleberry in everyone's faces and butting into the conversation with stuff about guinea pig poo, like the total idiot that he is.' She rolled her eyes as far back as it was possible for them to go without rolling out of her head altogether.

Good old Ty! I wished I'd been there. Jazz didn't notice my reaction; she was in too much of a tearing hurry to get me into her room. I almost tripped up the stairs. Once on the landing, she whirled into her room, her head twisting from side to side as though she were being tailed by a gang of evil mafia guys, and then yanked me through the door by my elbow, catching me off balance.

'Hey!'

133

'Shh!' she admonished, her finger to her lips. Ty might hear.' She closed the door quietly and firmly behind us and dragged a beanbag over to keep it shut − although I didn't think a beanbag would have much effect against the human cannonball that was Jazz's younger brother.

Jazz whizzed over to the far corner of the room, plonked herself on the floor and gestured wildly at me to sit with her.

I slumped down next to her and caught a strong whiff of something.

'Are you wearing perfume?' I asked disbelievingly.

Jazz scowled. 'Yeah. So? Anyway, listen − like I said, *he* came over with his mum.' Her voice had dropped to a half-whisper.

There was no use in complaining or trying to change the subject. Jazz had that flashing look in her eyes and that wide-stretched smile she reserved for occasions of extreme excitement, like the time

her dance class had won the regional champion-
ships and she had been chosen to go up on stage and
receive the cup.

'And?' I said, thinking I had to say something to
show I was listening.

'And you'll never guess what!' she replied,
pausing dramatically in what would have been
a build-up of tension. Except that as far as I was
concerned, there wasn't any.

'What?' I replied.

'His mum is a television producer and his dad
works in the music business!'

Oh no! This was possibly the worst news I had
had so far about this family. I could just about cope
with the fact that they were living in Kaboodle's
old house and had set my best friend's heart
aflutter with all the musical instruments they'd
moved in with, not to mention their son, but now
Jazz was telling me that the parents were her ticket
to fame and fortune! Well, that really put the lid on

it for me. The new family had it all. I was out of the picture. Case closed.

I sat hunched over, elbows on knees and head in hands, and half-listened as Jazz burbled away.

'The Meerleys know Pinkella from, like, ages ago? From when Pinkella was on TV all the time,' Jazz was saying in that know-it-all voice she'd used the day before when she'd told me their names.

'Pinkella? On telly?' I butted in. This was news to me, I thought irritably. She'd told us she'd been in films and plays and stuff, but on telly? 'Since when? I've never seen her in anything.'

'Yeah, well, it was, like, *way* before we were born, wasn't it?' Jazz said impatiently. 'Anyway, when Pinkella's house came up for rent the Meerleys were the first people she thought of. And this is where the REALLY cool stuff comes in,' Jazz finished. She bounced up, grabbed a newspaper from her desk and opened it in front of me with a flourish.

'Da-daaah!' she sang, beaming such an exaggerated smile I thought her face might actually split in two.

'What?' I asked. I was looking at a copy of the *Daily Ranter*, the paper that Dad used to write for. There had not been anything interesting to read in it when he had been responsible for most of the articles and I could not imagine that there would be anything interesting to read in it now that he wasn't.

'Since when have you been a loyal reader of the *Ranter*?' I asked, trying to sound cool while a wobbly feeling of unease seized my guts.

'Fiona showed it to me. Read it!' Jazz insisted, jabbing at the paper and thrusting it nearer.

Who's Got Talent? You Have!

the bold black type shouted.

Already I was not liking the sound of this.

137

Jazz pulled the paper impatiently out of my hands with a huff of exasperation and started to read out loud. I peered over her shoulder at the words.

'Have you got what it takes to star in the nation's favourite television show, *Who's Got Talent?* If so, Simon Cow and Danni Minnow want to meet you! Britain's biggest talent show is in town this Sunday 12th August, looking for the new star who'll get the once-in-a-lifetime opportunity to win a recording contract. Remember, it's all about a new voice and a new look, so don't forget to dress to impress! Make sure you join the crowds at the Pinkington Theatre at 8am sharp.

'Can you *believe* it?' Jazz finished in a squeak. She had not drawn breath once, and now she was clutching her hands to her chest and gazing at the ceiling in a dream-like stance, as if Prince Charming had just snogged her and made all her wishes come true. I shuddered.

'Oh. My. Goodness!' Jazz continued. 'This has *so* got to be the most exciting thing that has ever happened to me. In My. Whole. Boring. Life! They'll be here! In our dumb old town where nothing ever happens to anyone. And Fiona is the producer! She knows Simon and Danni and . . . and oh, everyone!' she finished in an exaggerated sigh, still gazing upwards as if a host of heavenly celebrities were about to be lowered down through the ceiling on a glittery pedestal right in front of us.

'Erm, yeah. It's cool,' I said quietly. Jazz always had this effect on me when she got overexcited about something. The louder she got, the quieter I became.

Jazz still hadn't noticed my reaction. She was now jabbing her finger at the newspaper and saying, 'So, what are we going to wear?'

What? Since when did *we* become involved?

'Er, sorry?' I stammered, playing for time.

'What are we going to wear?' Jazz repeated, suddenly sounding touchy. 'Come *on*, Bertie. Get with the programme! Haven't you worked it out yet? Fiona's the producer; I've met her; she likes me. I told her I was into the performing arts . . . Duh! It's obvious, isn't it?'

Oh dearie, dearie me with knobs on! Jazz was on a roll. And as usual it was all based on the assumption that, as ever, I would be happy to go along with her plans. It was always the same: Jazz snapped her fingers and I was supposed to jump to it and do what she said. I was getting pretty fed up with it all, to be honest.

But of course Jazz had not noticed my total lack of excitement. 'Tell you what, let's make a list, right? You like lists, don't you, Bertie?' I flinched. She was talking to me like I was her baby sister all of a sudden. 'Here.' She snatched a pad and pen from her desk and started scribbling and reading aloud as she wrote: 'What – I – Need – to – Dress – to – Impress . . .'

What I Need to Dress
to Impress

Tightest white jeans → →Tight!

Pink halter-neck top
with gold sequins

Pink and purple beads
Squillions of bangles
New Converse trainers with stars
on and new laces to match

Lip gloss

Fake nails - pink with silver hearts

What was it with these false nails? A sudden rush of anger welled in my throat.

'Sorry, Jazz, but I don't see what this show has got to do with you – or me – or the – what's their name? – *Meerleys*,' I said.

Jazz's face clouded dangerously. I stared back at her

while a dizzying sensation in the pit of my stomach gathered momentum like a distant thunderstorm.

'What are you talking about?' Jazz asked, her eyes narrowed. 'It's got EVERYTHING to do with us!'

I waited.

Jazz waggled her head at me as though I was the slowest train on the tracks and said slowly, for the benefit of my idiot-loony brain: 'I told you; Fiona is the producer. She can get us to the front of the queue.'

'How do you know *Fiona* can get us in? Have you asked her?' I felt myself squaring up to Jazz, even though part of my brain was telling me to stop, to slow down and let her have her moment in the sun.

Jazz faltered. 'I – I – it's just obvious. She's soooo lovely and I bet if I asked her it would be cool. Anyway, I am going to audition,' she ended abruptly.

I knew it. I tried to keep my voice level.

'So you haven't actually asked her yet? I mean, you haven't had a proper conversation about it?'

Jazz's face was growing bleaker by the minute. I watched it dawn on her that she hadn't thought this thing through.

'Why don't we just go and watch?' I tried to sound reasonable. I didn't want to upset my best mate, I told myself. 'Dad used to work for the *Ranter*, don't forget. Maybe he could sort us some good seats.'

Jazz flicked her braids out of her face and shot me a look of utter horror. '*He* can't come with us!' she gasped.

Admittedly, the idea of Dad rocking up to *Who's Got Talent?* in his naff jeans and faded sludge-coloured T-shirt was pretty horrific – even *I* knew that. But that didn't mean I was happy with Jazz's reaction. What had this Fiona got that my dad hadn't? (Apart from contacts in TV and the music business, I thought glumly.)

I squinted at the tiny writing in the newspaper that outlined the rules for the auditions, while a rollercoaster rocketed around somewhere inside me. I couldn't deal with all the different feelings this conversation was stirring up. On the one hand I wanted to scream at Jazz to shut up about this new family and the auditions, and to get a grip. On the other I wanted her to give me a hug and tell me nothing had changed and we were still best mates and by the way, here was a poster she'd been working on to help find Jaffa, and did I want to go out right now and stick copies up everywhere?

But soon Jazz was off on one again, conveniently sidestepping all my practical questions.

'So, like I said, what are *you* going to wear? I'm going to practise that new routine I'm learning in my Street Dance class, hence the jeans cos I'm doing the splits – not that great a look in a skirt and quite tricky to do too. Then again, maybe my white jeans will be too tight—'

'You can't,' I said quietly.

'What now?' Jazz said, one eyebrow arched.

'Jazz,' I said, taking her cue and adopting her you-are-not-on-Planet-Normal approach. 'You're eleven—'

'Twelve in three months!' she cut in defiantly.

'You're eleven,' I repeated. 'And you can't audition for *Who's Got Talent?* until you're sixteen.'

'Says who?' Jazz's confident expression wavered.

'Look.' I pointed at the small print which laid down the terms and conditions. 'It says here you have to be sixteen.'

'So? I could *look* sixteen if I got Aleisha to lend me some make-up,' she said airily.

I could not keep a lid on my emotions any longer. 'Yeah, like she's going to do that!' I rapped out, my voice laced with sarcasm and anger. Putting my head on one side, I talked up in a baby voice to an imaginary older sister: 'Oh, hi, Leesh. Can I have some of your make-up, please?' I looked down as if talking to a smaller person. 'Sure, Jazz. What for?' 'Well, I'm entering the auditions for *Who's Got Talent?* and I need to dress to impress.' 'Of course, darling little sister. Here, take the whole shebang, why don't you, and while you're at it why not borrow my favourite designer jeans?'

Jazz had her hands on her hips and her face was hardening into a fierce mask of fury.

I threw my hands up. 'OK! OK! But you know what I mean!' I shouted. 'She'd have a fit if she knew what you were planning – and she'd definitely tell your mum.'

Jazz sucked her cheeks in and wobbled her head at me. 'You just don't want me to have a chance of winning,' she said through clenched teeth. I didn't think I'd ever seen her look so scary. I should have known then to back down.

But instead I did something really stupid. I couldn't help it. I don't even know where it came from – it burst out of me like bubblegum popping in my mouth.

I laughed.

It was just the idea that Jazz could actually believe that an eleven-year-old who sang like a strangled canary had the slightest chance of winning 'the nation's favourite talent show' and be on television – and get a recording contract!

Jazz, predictably, did not find the idea as amusing as I did.

'You, Bertie Fletcher, need to seriously get a life. And I mean *seriously*. You need to grow up. All this bonkers utter RUBBISH about pets and kittens and fluffy little hamster–wamsters. I mean how old ARE you exactly? We're not at Junior School any more, Bertie. We'll be nearly teenagers this time next year. You need to shape up your act, girl, or you are going to be doing time with the Losers of Loserville from here to the end of eternity. And I for one will not be hanging around to watch *that* happen.'

And she spun on her heel, her beads thwacking against her flushed cheeks, and marched out, slamming her door behind her, leaving me staring at the newspaper article and feeling as though she had just knocked all the life out of me.

147

10

Petless and Friendless

Some holiday this was turning out to be. I blundered down the stairs, swiping furiously at my wet, tear-streaked face and pushed past Ty who was standing in the hall, gawping at me and waving a long-suffering Huckleberry in the air.

'Ber-tiiie,' he whined. 'Jazz just called Huckleberry a tail-less lettuce-munching rat!'

'S-sorry, Ty. Gotta go,' I mumbled, letting myself out of the house and running down the street before Jazz's mum or sister could spot me and make me sit down with Jazz and 'try to sort it all out'.

All I could think was how much distance I wanted to put between me and Jazz.

Petless and Friendless

How could she have said those things? We had always been mates. OK, so we didn't get on one hundred per cent of the time, but she'd never been so hurtful before. What was I going to do now? It had always been Jazz and Bertie, Bertie and Jazz. I wished I had Kaboodle to run home to – that gorgeous, soft, clever little kitten who always had some words of wisdom and a loud jet-engine purr to make me feel better. He certainly would have had some sharp, witty comments up his whiskers when it came to Jazz. But Kaboodle had gone. And Jaffa too. And Dad was working.

I thought of Jazz and how she too was probably in tears right this minute because I had laughed at her. I should have felt bad about that, I supposed. But why should I feel sorry for her? She had a mum to cuddle her when she was down, a big sister to give her advice. She even had a guinea pig in the family.

I had no one.

I was wallowing in the deep end of my own personal pool of misery and running along at full tilt with my hair flying in my face, so I didn't see someone coming the other way. And I ran right into them.

'Uh – oh, sorry!' I muttered, keeping my face hidden behind a curtain of mad-as-a-mongoose hair.

'Er, it's OK,' said the someone.

I wiped my face on the back of my sleeve and moved to one side to get past.

The someone moved in the same direction and we bumped into one another again. I felt heat rise to my face.

'Sorry!' I almost shouted it this time. I just wanted to get home.

Then I sensed a hand on my arm and glanced up sharply.

'Hey, you OK? You look as though you've been crying.'

Oh. No. Holy Stromboli with grated cheese

and extra salami. It was only *him* wasn't it? Prince Charming himself.

'I – I'm sorry. It's none of my business. I'm Fergus, by the way – we're neighbours, I think.'

I pursed my lips to stop myself from coming out with any words that I might live to regret for the rest of my life.

Fergus was taller than me. He had to stoop to try and hold my gaze while I shuffled uncomfortably and tried to flick my hair back over my eyes. I couldn't think of anything to say and wished he would stop staring at me like that. Apart from anything else, it made it difficult for me to get a proper look at him.

'How old are you?' I blurted out.

WHAT DID I SAY THAT FOR? We weren't in Reception any more! Next thing I'll be asking him if he wants to be my friend. Actually, scrap that. That's one thing I would definitely *not* be asking him.

Fergus grinned. I noticed, through my hair-curtain, that he had very white even teeth. And *his* hair was actually really glossy and quite an unusual dark red, which glinted in the sunlight – what you'd call auburn. I felt even more of a hot and dirty mess.

In fact, I felt like I was running a temperature. I wished the pavement would split in two and that some alien life form would emerge and drag me down into the depths.

'Thirteen. Why? How old are you?' Fergus was saying.

I was so shocked I forgot to stay hidden behind my fringe. My eyes were doing their best to leap out of their sockets, but I did my best to restrain them. *Thirteen?* Bang went Jazz's dreams of Prince Charming leading her up into the dizzying heights of fame and fortune!

'I'm eleven – nearly twelve,' I added, immediately biting my lip and thinking how utterly dumb that sounded. Why didn't I just say 'eleven' and be done with it?

'Oh. Right – I thought you might be older than that,' Fergus said, his smooth face going a bit pink. 'It's just – er – your friend Jazz told me she was thirteen and I guess I thought you might be in the same year as her.'

I was finding it incredibly difficult to speak like a normal human being. Jazz was unbelievable. But for some weird reason, I couldn't allow myself to drop her in it and tell Fergus the truth.

'So. I guess we'll be in the same school in September,' he was babbling on.

'Yeah, probably.'

I'd calmed down slightly now, what with all this bizarre conversation, and I realized I didn't feel like crying any more. I sniffed loudly.

'So, er, what are you into?' Fergus said, kicking at a leaf on the pavement.

'What?' I said. What kind of a question was that, for goodness sake?

153

'Well, like, your friend Jazz is into music and dancing and stuff – she told me all about it—'

'I bet she did,' I muttered.

'Eh?'

'I said, "That sounds like Jazz!"' I fibbed extra-brightly.

'Yeah, so – are you into music?' he persisted, peering down at me through his floppy fringe.

I picked at some loose threads on the sleeve of my T-shirt. 'Kind of. Not really. I mean, it's OK, but it's not my *thing*,' I said with a slight sneer. 'I'm not in a successful band or anything.'

I knew I should be trying to be nice to this boy. He was only making conversation. He was probably a bit lonely if he'd moved a long way from all his friends. And I knew what lonely felt like. But it was all that stuff about Jazz: I couldn't help it.

'Oh, right. You've heard about the band . . . Actually, it doesn't exist any more. We had to split when I moved,' Fergus said. He looked sad sudden-

154

ly. Then he blurted out suddenly, 'Sorry, enough about me. I should let you go. Erm – hope you don't mind me asking though, but is everything OK? Only, you were crying, like I said, and—'

All at once I was fed up with this freaky chit-chat with a boy I had never even wanted to meet in the first place. I didn't care about his band. I didn't care about him. I snapped. 'Not that it's any of your business, but *animals* are really "my thing"; not music, not *Summer School Dance Camp*, not Zeb Acorn, not Street Dance – *animals*. And if you absolutely have to know why I was crying, it's cos I've lost my cat and she's only little, so it's kind of upsetting.'

I had been trying to keep my eyes fixed firmly on the pavement during this whole tirade, so that I didn't embarrass myself by bursting into tears again, but a sharp gasp from Fergus made me start.

'What?' I asked, looking up.

Fergus was frowning and chewing his lip.

'Have *you* seen her?' I pressed him.

'I'm not sure, but . . . You say she's little. How little?' Fergus asked, his dark blue eyes clouding over. Why was he suddenly so concerned about my kitten?

'We-ell, size-wise she's about this big.' I showed him with my hands exactly how tiny my little Jaffa was. About the size of a grapefruit – I could still hold her in one hand. The last time I'd held her, anyway. 'But we don't know exactly how old she is. She was given to us, you see. By – by the lady who owns the house you're living in, as it happens.'

Fergus smiled. 'Oh, Fenella Pinkington.'

I found myself smiling too. 'Yeah. Pinkella!'

Fergus laughed. 'Great nickname – wish I'd thought of that! Makes sense when you see the walls and carpets. Mum'll crack up when I tell her.'

I was horrified. 'You can't tell your *mum*! She might tell Pink— I mean, Ms Pinkington, and I'd hate that. She was really nice to me,' I tailed off, pathetically.

Fergus shrugged. I could tell he thought I was a right doofus. 'So – your kitten,' he prompted.

'So?' Was he humouring me?

'Tell me what she's like. Apart from being small.'

'I – well, she's mega-cute. I called her Jaffa cos she's gingery-orange. Made me think of Jaffa Cakes? Oh, and she's a bit white too. And she seemed really happy with us to start with, and then we had to take her to the vet for her jabs and stuff, and ever since then—'

'Sorry,' said Fergus, interrupting my stream of babble. 'Did you say she was ginger?' He was looking anxious again.

'Yeah, unusual for a female cat, I know,' I said airily, hoping I sounded knowledgeable.

'No, it's not that. It's just, I . . .' He faltered, suddenly looking ill at ease.

'Yes?'

'No, really. It's nothing. Er, listen, are you doing anything right now? Do you want to maybe go to

157

the park or something?'

Where did that come from? I thought, my forehead creasing into a frown. Why would he want to
go to the park? With me? He was definitely wind-
ing me up now.

'No thanks,' I said firmly. 'I need to look for Jaffa
and I don't think she could have gone all that way.'

He chewed his lip and then said in a totally over-
the-top fake careless manner: 'It's OK. I only asked
as I was going to the park anyway. Might call on
your mate Jazz and ask her if she's free.'

'Fine,' I said, turning on my heel. 'See you
around.'

'Yeah, see you!' Fergus called out.

'Oh.' I swivelled back. 'And if you do see a small
ginger kitten, you will let me know, won't you?'

Fergus glanced away quickly. 'Uh-huh.' He nodded casually. Then stuffing his hands deep into his
pockets, he turned round very slowly and slouched
off in the direction of Jazz's house.

11

Now We're Talking!

Dad was in the hall, beaming all over his face when I got in.

'What's up?' I asked gloomily.

'Look who's here!' he said, gesturing towards the sitting room with a 'Daa-daaaa!' and a flourish of his hands, as if he'd just pulled a white rabbit out of a top hat.

Actually, it was better than that.

'JAFFSIE!' I yelled, my whole face lighting up with joy. I stopped myself just in time from running towards her and frightening the life out

of her, and instead I tiptoed up to my little kitten and scooped her into my arms for a gentle cuddle. 'Where have you been?' I whispered, rubbing my nose softly against her fur.

She whipped round and sank her tiny, needle-sharp teeth into my hand. 'Miaaaaaow! None of Bertie's business.'

'Wh—aaaaaa?' I nearly dropped her.

'Hey, that was some noise! Did she scratch you?' Dad asked, leaping to my side.

'I – yes, but it wasn't . . .' I stammered. She *had* spoken to me, hadn't she? Or had I imagined it in my excitement?

'Grrrrrooowl!' Jaffa let out a low warning snarl.

And then (I was absolutely sure of this) I heard her say something, so soft that it came out in a hiss: 'Don't you be telling that man *nothin'*.'

I gasped.

'She's hurt you, hasn't she?' Dad said, looking concerned. 'Give her to me,' he went on, stretching out his arms. 'Blimey! Who would have thought such a tiny cat could—'

'No, no, it's fine,' I said, thinking quickly. 'I think she must be hungry. I'll go and get her something to eat.'

Dad shook his head. 'You know what? I tried giving her something when she came trotting in just now, but she wasn't interested.'

'What did you give her?'

'That kitten food, of course. What else was I supposed to offer? A prawn cocktail?'

'Kitten food yucky. Prawns . . . *purrrrr* . . . scrumlummmmtious.'

There it was again!

'I – I'm going to try something else,' I said, backing out of the sitting room. 'I think we should give her a proper treat to welcome her home. Actually, *have* we got any prawns?' I asked, as casually as I could.

Jaffa started purring so noisily at this, I was

completely positive that she had understood what I'd just said. I was intent on getting away from Dad by now. I had to go to my room so that I could talk to Jaffa. Maybe once I got her on her own we could have a proper conversation and she'd tell me where she'd been the past few days.

'We have, but . . .' said Dad, sounding unsure. 'Hey, I think I might just ring Bex at the pet shop to ask her if she thinks it's safe to give Jaffa rich food.'

'Fine,' I cut in quickly. This was just the diversion I needed, even if it involved 'Bex', I thought irritably. 'We'll be in the kitchen.'

Dad was already dialling the number for Paws for Thought. I vaguely wondered why he hadn't needed to look it up in the telephone directory, but was too preoccupied with the purring bundle in my arms to follow this thought through.

I scurried to the kitchen and shut the door behind me, then, lifting Jaffa to my face, I said, 'So tell me, am I imagining it? Or can you really talk?'

Now We're Talking!

Jaffa's icy blue eyes closed in a slow blink and then she stopped purring and in a tiny muffled voice said, 'Of course me can talk. You ninny.'

I laughed out loud. 'Ha! I knew you could. I knew Kaboodle wouldn't have left me with a cat that couldn't talk!'

Jaffa's ears went flat and she hissed in annoyance. 'All cats talk, silly-billy. Humans too busy rushy-rushy to notice.'

I frowned. 'That's not true,' I said. 'I've been trying to get you to talk to me ever since you arrived.' Jaffa lifted one paw and examined it absent-mindedly before spreading out her toes to wash in between them.

'Oh, for heaven's sake!' I blurted out. 'I know you cats like to think before you act and wash before you think and all that, but I think I'm entitled to an explanation, don't you?'

Jaffa wriggled and said tetchily, 'Me want go down!'

163

I tutted, but set her down gently on the table and drew up a chair so that we could face each other more easily. 'So?' I persisted. 'Why didn't you talk to me before now?'

'Like the horrid iron-claw lady say – kittens not talk right away,' she said, with an edge to her voice that seemed to imply that I really was incredibly stupid.

I frowned, puzzled. Horrid iron-claw lady?

'Me not going there again. Ever,' Jaffa added emphatically.

Aaaah! Light dawned in my dim and befuddled brain. 'You mean the vet?' I said. 'That wasn't her claws: we took you to the vet for an injection!' I almost laughed, but saw that Jaffa was giving me an if-you-were-a-mouse-I-would-kill-you-right-here-and-now look. 'I'm sorry,' I said hastily. 'I really am. I know injections are nasty, but it's only so you don't get sick.'

'Me nearly *was* sick after nasty lady stuck claws

164

in me,' Jaffa said, her voice getting more audible the more indignant she became. She thrust her tiny pink nose in the air. 'And there was horrid long twisty-turny scary creature too.'

The snake! I hadn't even realized Jaffa had noticed it in all the excitement.

I thought she was about to turn her back on me in a sulk, but she opened one eye and then said, 'You *sure* I not go again to this – *vet* person . . .?'

I chewed my lip. I couldn't really promise that, could I? What about the follow-up vaccinations Dad had mentioned? And what if Jaffa ever got sick or needed an operation or something?

'There's nothing to worry about, Jaffa,' I said in as soothing a voice as I could manage.

Jaffa opened her other eye and stretched her mouth into what looked strangely like a smile. She purred long and loud and nuzzled her soft head against my hand. 'All right,' she said. 'But who is the "Jaffa" you keep sayin'?'

165

I giggled. 'That's you! It's the name I chose for you.'

Jaffa sat back on her haunches, her eyes half closed as if she were thinking hard. 'No, no, no . . .' she said, shaking her head slightly. She turned swiftly and gave her shoulder a lick. 'Me Perdita. Mum said.'

Panic lurched in my stomach. Did Jaffa even know that she'd been taken from her mum? She was still such a tiny baby. Maybe she didn't realize? What had Kaboodle told her? Was that why she'd disappeared for so long – to try and find her mum?

'Er, yes, that's what your mum called you, but we humans are muppets when it comes to cat names,' I improvised, remembering the disparaging way Kaboodle used to talk about my human failings. 'We, er, we can never pronounce names like Per-per-wotsit. So we always give our cats a new name when they come to live with us. So you're Jaffa,' I explained.

Now We're Talking!

Jaffa stood up quickly and
arched her back in alarm. 'Liv-
in' with you? Me not stayin'
here *all* of the times!' she said.
'Me come and go when me wants.
That is what cats does. Mum said.'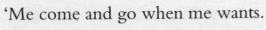

A lump rose in my throat. I put out my hand and
tried to stroke her to reassure her, but she hissed
and backed away. 'Jaffa,' I said gently, 'you do live
here. This is where your home is – and your food,'
I added, thinking this might persuade her.

'But me gets food in other place too,' she said,
puzzled. 'And me not called Jaffa there.'

'Er – what other place?' I asked, the lump in my
throat growing larger by the second.

'Other place,' Jaffa repeated, her head on one side
as if shrugging. 'Prawns in other place,' she added.
And I was positive she smiled as she said this.

'Jaffa,' I said slowly, 'I need to know where this
other place is.'

'Why?'

'Because – because I need to tell the people there that you're my cat.'

'Why?'

'Because they have to know that they shouldn't feed you.'

'Why?'

'Because, for a start, we're not even sure you should be eating prawns yet.'

'Why?'

I gritted my teeth. This was like talking to Jazz's little brother.

'Because you're only small, that's why. And it's my duty to look after you and feed you and love you.'

I gathered her into my hands before she could let out another 'why' and held her close to my face.

She softly licked my cheek with her pink sand-paper tongue.

Now We're Talking!

'All right,' she said. 'Me stays here if you is the food-person.'

Phew! Thank goodness, I thought, letting her rub her face against my cheek. She seemed to have got the message. Maybe everything was going to be all right now that Jaffa and I could understand one another.

How wrong could I be?

12

Collared!

Dad came into the kitchen just as I had found the prawns in the fridge and was about to set them in front of Jaffa.

'Stop!' he cried, rushing over and snatching the dish away. 'I spoke to Bex and she said it wasn't a good idea. She said you have to introduce new food slowly in case Jaffa gets sick.' I bristled. 'Yeah, well, "Bex" would say that, wouldn't she?' I was getting really fed up with Dad quoting that woman all the time, like she was some kind of pet guru. I'd promised Jaffa the prawns. If I went back on my promise, she wouldn't trust me and might try and run off again.

Dad frowned. 'Tone of Voice, young lady,' he admonished. 'I think Bex knows what she's talking about. She's got cats herself, you know, and she's run Paws for Thought for ages – ten years, I think she said.'

'Good for her,' I muttered, but catching the increasingly grumpy look on Dad's face, I rolled my eyes and said, 'OK, OK. What about cream then? Or a tiny bit of tuna?'

'Me luuuuurve crrrrream!' Jaffa purred, rubbing her head against my ankle.

I started in surprise. Who were these people who were giving her prawns and cream? I wished I could get my hands on them. If Jaffa only got boring old kitten food at our place, she was sure to go off again in search of something more tasty. And if what 'Bex' said was true, they were setting me up for a whole bunch of problems: what if Jaffa got sick and I had to take her back to the vet even sooner than I had to for the injections? She would never forgive me, and then I'd lose her for good.

Dad was chattering away at me as these thoughts bounced around inside my brain. I was so steaming angry – with the mystery catnapping people, with Dad and with blinking 'Bex' – that I didn't catch everything he'd said and only heard: 'So I think you could give her a tiny amount, but only as a treat.'

'Sorry?' I said, irritably.

Dad sighed and shook his head. 'I *said* you can give her one prawn as a treat and then maybe every day we could introduce a little more variety into her diet.'

'Right,' I said abruptly, unimpressed.

'OK, well, "Thanks, Dad, for finding all that information for me." "You're welcome, Bertie. Any time."' He glared at me, but I busied myself with chopping one measly prawn up into lots of tiny bits so that it looked like more, and arranged it on a saucer for Jaffa.

Dad huffed and finally left the room when it became clear I was not in a chatty mood.

'Maybe you'll cheer up now Jaffa's back?' he called over his shoulder.

Maybe, I thought. But the rate at which Jaffa had wolfed down the prawn and the pleading way she was now looking up at me left me with a sinking feeling that I had rather a big competition on my hands.

It turned out my sinking feeling was not just that. It was fact. Jaffa disappeared again the next day while Dad was hanging out the washing.

'Dad!' I yelled at him. 'How could you have left the door open AGAIN? After all I've just been through.'

Dad's face darkened. 'Don't talk to me like that,' he warned. 'I think you're being a little bit dramatic, Bertie. It's not as if Jaffa didn't come back, is it? And you're going to have to get used to her coming and going as she gets older. Listen,' he said,

179

holding up a hand as I started to protest, 'I'm getting fed up with all the SAS tactics necessary to keep Jaffa inside, to be honest. How do you think I am supposed to do the laundry if I keep having to close the door behind me? I need to be able to come and go without watching my back all the time.'

'You could have shut Jaffa in another room first!' I wasn't going to be shouted down that easily. Dad didn't know what I knew about the 'other place'. And I could hardly tell him, as I didn't have any proof other than the fact that my kitten had told me.

'Bertie, I'm sick of this. If you become this frazzled every time Jaffa goes out for a pee or to chase a mouse or something, maybe you're just not cut out for cat-ownership,' he snapped.

I froze. 'B-but you love Jaffsie,' I said in a quiet voice, not unlike Jaffa's own.

Dad's shoulders relaxed and he came over and gave me a hug. 'Of course I do, darling,' he said.

174

'And I'm sorry, that came out wrong because you shouted at me and I lost my rag. But, Bertie love, you've got to try and get some perspective on this. Jaffa's not a dog: you can't keep her on a lead. I know we're supposed to try and keep her in, but if she's as determined as this to get out, I don't see what we can do. She'll come back again, I promise.'

I drew back from his hug and gave him a sceptical look.

'And if she doesn't come back right away,' Dad said wearily, 'I'll go looking for her myself, even if it means knocking on people's doors, OK? Now, go and do something useful like tidying your bedroom – or give Jazz a call and sort out your differences, eh? I've got to get on.'

I grunted and left the room while he whisked around, tidying up the kitchen. I went into the sitting room, grabbed a book and flopped on to our low window sill. It wasn't the comfiest of seats, but it meant I could pretend to read while keeping an eye out on the road to see if Jaffa was darting between our neighbours' houses.

I tried to distract myself by reading a couple of lines of my book, but I'd never been much of a reader and it took too much concentration to get back into the story. Besides, my bum hurt, perching on the window sill like that. I couldn't settle. I threw the book down and pulled out my mobile to check my messages.

Nothing. No voicemails either. Jazz wasn't going to be making the first move then, I thought miserably.

I toyed with the idea of going round there on the pretext of asking if she'd seen Fergus. It might have been fun to see the look on her face if I casually mentioned that I'd met him and that he'd asked me to the park. But I knew where that would lead, and I wasn't up for a fight. I thought about saying I'd help her get into the auditions for *Who's Got Talent?* That would make her sit up and take notice of me. But then I didn't exactly have any grand plans about how I was going to make that happen.

As these crazy thoughts fizzed and popped in my mind, I paced around the room, circling the carpet the way Dad does in his study when he's stuck on a scene and doesn't know what to write. I was making my third or fourth tour of the room when I heard a soft 'Meeeeew' from outside.

'Jaffa?' I called, rushing out to the hall.

'Meeeeeew! Me locked out!'

'It's OK. Bertie's here!' I cried, pathetically. I opened the front door to see my tiny cat sitting on the doormat, licking her chest and twitching her head round as if she was irritated by something.

'What's up, Jaffsie?' I crooned as I bent down to pick her up. 'You having a nice little wash?' I kissed her gently. That's odd, I thought – she smells funny. Kind of lemony. It reminded me of something, but I couldn't think what. My fingers brushed against something rough on the back of her neck and there was a tinkling sound.

'What's this?'

I held her away from me so I could get a good look at her.

'Itchy . . .' Jaffa mumbled as she continued washing.

I gasped. There, around my beautiful kitten's soft, fluffy neck, was a hideous, glittery purple collar! It looked huge against Jaffa's small frame, and it glimmered and shimmered like a dress a ballroom dancer or an ice skater might wear. It was disgusting.

'Yeee-uuck!' I howled in horror. 'Where on earth did this come from?'

Jaffa jumped and howled back, her ears flat and her eyes bulging. 'No shouty at me!' she miaowed. 'Me didn't do it!'

I chewed my bottom lip. 'I know. Of course you didn't. I didn't mean to upset you. But,' I hesitated, 'who did?'

Jaffa turned her head slightly away. 'Not telling,' she said stiffly.

I felt a knot of frustration forming in my stomach. I wanted to scream at Jaffa to tell me about this other person she was making herself at home with, but I made myself stay calm. After all, as Dad said, Jaffa had at least come back. And it didn't look as though she liked the collar all that much, the way she was pulling and licking at it. So maybe she was coming round to the idea that my house was the best option. Well, I was going to make sure I sent a very clear message to the 'other place'. I was going to get rid of that collar right away.

'Jaffa,' I said quietly 'shall we see if there are any nice treats in the kitchen?'

I carried her down the hall. Forget what Dad and 'Bex' said about introducing new food gradually, I thought.

'Jaffa!' Just my luck, Dad was still in the kitchen. 'See, Bertie? Told you she'd come back. Hey, what's that round her neck?' He came over to gawp at the gross disco-collar.

I raised an eyebrow. 'What does it look like?' I was willing him to go away so that I could get rid of the thing as quickly as possible without alarming Jaffa.

'You didn't buy her that, did you?' Dad was like a dog with a bone – he was not going to let this thing go. 'Where did you get it?'

'Why that man so crazy mad?' Jaffa mewed.

I laughed.

'Bertie! Don't laugh at me when I'm talking to you. Answer my question,' Dad demanded.

I sucked my cheeks in. 'Wasn't me. Jaffa just came back wearing it and I now fully intend to get rid of it. But first of all I need a treat to distract her.'

I marched past Dad to the utensils pot and snatched a pair of kitchen scissors and then I opened the fridge, intending to grab another prawn and feed it to Jaffa while I cut the collar off.

'Hold it right there,' Dad said. 'I don't know

what's going on, but you're not giving her any more prawns. If you want to distract her, give her a cat biscuit.'

'Me don't like them bikkit things,' Jaffa whined.

'She doesn't like them,' I told Dad stroppily.

Dad crouched down beside me. 'Since when?' he said.

'Since for ever!' mewled Jaffa.

'*She doesn't like them!*' I repeated loudly, trying to cover Jaffa's whining. 'One more prawn isn't going to kill her.'

Dad got up, looking at me and Jaffa as if we were both loop-the-loop. 'Okaaaay. Don't mind me. I just live here.' And, thank goodness, he left me to it, muttering about 'moody daughters' being bad enough but 'moody kittens' being another thing altogether.

'Jaffa!' I hissed, once Dad was out of earshot. 'What's going on? You run away to goodness knows where and won't tell me, you refuse to eat the food we've bought you, then you're off again and you come back wearing a *rank* new collar and won't tell me who's given it to you, and to make matters worse it feels like you've only found your voice to use it against me! I – I love you, you know,' I faltered. This was not the approach I had wanted to take.

Jaffa let out a mini kitten-sized sigh and said huffily with her pretty pink nose in the air, 'Me not talking till me gets prawn.'

'Sorry?' I stammered.

'Praaaaaaaaaaawn!' She let out a long plaintive mew.

I was worried the noise might bring Dad running back again, so I hastily staggered to my feet. 'OK, OK! Hang on a second.'

Jaffa stuck her nose higher in the air and said nothing.

I set her down on the work surface and got a prawn out of the fridge, then I picked the scissors up again and turned back to Jaffa, making 'Here, kitty-kitty' noises for Dad's benefit in case he had his study door open.

'Me not Kitty-kitty,' Jaffa pouted.

I chose not to react to this and held out the prawn.

Jaffa's whiskers twitched at the fishy aroma, and she edged slowly forward, looking as though she was creeping up on an unsuspecting mouse and about to pounce. I would have thought it was funny if I hadn't been so worried about what she might do next.

'Mmm! Yummy-yum-yum in my tum-tum,' Jaffa purred, her dainty little pink tongue licking a piece of fish from the edge of the bowl.

'Glad you like it,' I said, using the distraction of the food to slide the scissor blade swiftly under the truly repulsive purple collar and give it a satisfyingly crunchy SNIP. Jaffa was enjoying the prawn so much, she didn't even notice. One point to me, Mr or Mrs Whoever-you-are Catnapper person, I thought to myself with a sneer.

Kitten Wars

Finally Jaffa gave a content-
ed little yawn, showing
every one of her minus-
cule pointy white teeth, and
set to work licking her paws and
washing behind her ears.

I couldn't wait another second. 'Jaffa,' I
said carefully, 'now you've eaten, can you please
answer my questions?'

Jaffa stopped in mid-chest-lick and blinked at
me. 'Questions?' she asked blankly.

'Who gave you the collar?' I asked as calmly as
possible.

'Nice prawn lady,' Jaffa answered smugly.

Aha! So now at least I knew it was a lady.

I carried Jaffa back into the sitting room and settled
down in an armchair near the window for a cuddle.
So, I thought, as I picked up my book again and
flicked through the pages idly, if I wanted to find
out who was trying to steal my cat, I would have to

look for a woman who had enough money to spend on showering Jaffa with prawns and who thought accessorizing a cat with glitter was a good idea. I racked my brains but couldn't think of any woman who matched that description in our cul-de-sac. Hey, maybe it was a girl – one who liked purple . . .

No, it couldn't be! Jazz wasn't interested in animals.

Was she?

I shivered. Jazz was the only person I could think of who would imagine a cat would look great in such a horrible collar. The last time I'd seen her she'd flown off the handle at me for being worried about Jaffa, and I hadn't spoken to her since Jaffa had come back . . . Was my once best mate now so angry with me that she would stoop this low?

I stared out of the window, my brain locked in freeze mode.

And then I spotted Fergus Meerley walking up his front drive, and I had an idea.

13

Something Fishy

I left Jaffa snoozing on the sofa and shouted to Dad that I was going out.

'Where?' he shouted back.

'New neighbours!' I called, then I scooted out of the front door before he had a chance to pass comment.

I ran over the road to number 15 and had my hand on the doorbell when I realized what a stupid thing I was doing. Who did I think I was, rushing over uninvited, and to a boy's house at that? It was the kind of thing Jazz might do, I thought ruefully, as I backed away from the door and prepared to make a run for it.

Something Fishy

Too late – the door was flung open and there was Fergus, peering through that ultra-shiny fringe of his. He reddened.

'Oh, hi. It's you,' he said.

My heart sank into my boots. He'd been expecting it to be someone else, hadn't he? No prizes for guessing who. Oh well, no getting out of it now: I would have to speak to him. He looked a bit like Zeb Acorn, I thought. He was wearing a black T-shirt with a zig-zaggy white motif on it and super-skinny black jeans with a pair of beaten-up black Converses. I couldn't help admitting Jazz was right: he did look cool.

I shook my head angrily. I didn't want to think about Jazz.

'Yeah, it's me,' I said. Doh! What a numpty.

'Er, d'you wanna come in?' he mumbled, looking at the floor. Not exactly the world's warmest invitation, especially since he wasn't even moving to one side to let me pass.

'I – well, OK,' I muttered.

This was such a bad idea. I was in way over my head. I'd rushed over here on a whim, thinking I was going to be able to enlist Fergus's help in finding out what Jazz was up to with Jaffa. And now I had no plan of what to say or how to behave. What had I thought I was going to ask: 'So, when you went round to Jazz's did you see a small ginger cat?' Not exactly subtle. At best he'd think I was a control-freak pet-mad baby, obsessed with my fluffy-wuffy kitten; at worst he'd think I was a one hundred per cent loser loony-case who'd got lost on her way out of Loserville and was too much of a loony to be allowed back in again.

'So, did you, like, find your cat?' Fergus reluctantly stepped to one side and gestured for me to come in.

Great. He did think I was a pet-mad control freak. 'Y-yes,' I stammered, fiddling with one of my curls till it got so tightly wrapped round my finger I realized in panic that it was stuck. I pretended to scratch my ear. 'And, er, no,' I added. 'Actually, that's what I came to talk to you about.'

Fergus looked at though I'd just slapped him in the face. 'Oh.' His eyes kept flicking down the hall towards the kitchen. Then it dawned on me: was Jazz there?

I felt cold despite the summer heat. I disentangled my finger and rubbed my arms. What if she was there? I wasn't ready to talk to her yet. Especially not in front of Fergus. I backed away and said, 'Actually, it really doesn't matter. Jaffa came back and then she went away again, but she's back now. It's OK. I don't know why I came round. Sorry to have bother—'

'Hey, hey, slow down,' Fergus said, putting his hand on my shoulder and then immediately withdrawing it as if he'd burned his fingers. 'I – listen, start from the beginning,' he said. He sounded kinder, but he was still looking shiftily in the

189

direction of the kitchen.

'She's not here, is she?' I blurted out.

'Who?' Fergus said – rather quickly, I noticed.

'Jazz,' I said.

I wasn't prepared for his reaction. He laughed. Long and loud and raucously, almost as though he were relieved.

'N-n-no, no no!' he gasped. Then, catching sight of my puzzled face he said, 'Sorry, it's just . . . I'm not exactly Jazz's favourite person at the moment.'

'Oh,' I said. Disappointment washed over me. Fergus wasn't going to be much use to me if he'd fallen out with Jazz as well. 'That's a shame,' I added lamely.

'It is?' Fergus asked, suddenly looking rather disappointed himelf.

'Yes. I was kind of hoping you'd be able to do something for me, you see,' I said, feeling a bit more confident now that Fergus seemed to be relaxing slightly.

Something Fishy

He gave a wry smile. 'If it's to do with Jazz, I doubt it. You know I was going round to see her when you and I met?' he asked, flushing again.

I nodded. Wow, Jazz had certainly got under his skin, I thought, watching the colour spread across his cheeks.

'Well, she wanted to know all about *Who's Got Talent?*, my mum's the producer, you see.' Don't I know it! 'Jazz went on and on at me to talk to Mum about getting her into the auditions.' Poor Fergus, he was looking really uncomfortable now. 'I had to tell her, Bertie. It's just not possible. You have to be—'

'Sixteen, I know,' I cut in. 'I told her that myself. But the thing about Jazz is, she doesn't understand the word 'no'. Unless she's using it herself,' I added quietly.

Fergus nodded. 'Yeah, I kind of worked that one out,' he said miserably. 'So I'm really sorry, Bertie. I'd love to be able to help you, but . . .' he tailed off, spreading his hands out and shrugging in a help-less gesture.

My face must have matched his at that moment, because for a split second he seemed to relent and said, 'What was it you wanted me to do anyway?'

I sighed. I may as well tell him, I thought. I've come this far.

'The thing is, Jazz and I had an argument the other day, and it coincided with Jaffa disappear-ing for the first time. And things have happened to Jaffa while she's been away which have led me to suspect that Jazz is somehow involved.' I cringed inwardly as I heard myself sounding like someone out of a TV police drama. I swallowed and ploughed on: 'For instance, she turned up today wearing a collar – a purple sparkly one! It was utterly gross and frankly exactly the kind of hideous accessory Jazz would think was "pop-tastic". Probably the kind of thing she'd wear herself to a *WGT?* audition, given half the chance,' I added sourly.

Something Fishy

The whole time I'd been speaking, Fergus's facial expression had changed from kindly interest to out-and-out shock, mingled with a dash of worried frowning along the way. It was good to see he was on my side.

'So, I was wondering if you'd seen any signs of a kitten while you were round there? Or maybe she'd mentioned having a cat? And if so, I was kind of hoping you might be able to persuade her that—'

'FERGIE!' A high-pitched voice rang down the hall. Fergus's look of shock intensified into one of complete stomach-crunching horror. 'Fergie?' the voice repeated. It was coming towards us from up-stairs. 'Who's that you're talking to? If it's one of the neighbours, ask them if they've seen Muffin, can you?'

Muffin? I looked at Fergus, my mouth turned down and eyebrows raised in a question. He wasn't looking at me, though. He'd pulled me by the arm and was propelling me to the front door, his other hand already on the door handle.

'Hey!' I protested.

'Aren't you going to introduce us?'

Fergus froze. He let his hand fall from my arm, but kept a tight hold on the door handle, as if he were trying to steady himself.

A woman about my dad's age was eyeing me with a mixture of bewilderment and distaste. My stomach did several back-flips. There was something distinctly scary about her. And there was a strong citrusy scent coming from her that was unsettlingly familiar.

'Fergie,' she snapped, looking me up and down. 'Why didn't you answer me? Didn't you hear me calling you? Or were you too busy chatting to . . .' She broke off and looked pointedly at me.

'B–B–Bertie,' I faltered.

I couldn't help noticing she was a real yummy mummy – neat little purple cardigan with tiny embroidered flowers and sequinny bits around the shoulder; short (but not too short) skirt and tights that were a dark purple that I reluctantly noticed were a great match with the cardi. Not a hair of her smooth reddish-brown mane was a millimetre out of place. No wonder Jazz had been seduced. A woman who liked clothes, and purple clothes too – a sure-fire way to Jazz's heart. And that hair! She would have been beautiful if she hadn't been so unfriendly.

I shuffled awkwardly, suddenly painfully aware of the fact that my own tangled mop hadn't seen a hairbrush for a couple of days and that my jeans had mud on one knee from earlier when I had been crawling around looking for Jaffa under bushes.

'Sorry, Mum,' Fergus muttered. 'Bertie and I were just about to go out.'

'Hmmm, getting to know all the *girls* in the area, aren't you, darling?' she said archly. 'So, Beryl,' she turned to me. 'You're the little girl from over the road, aren't you? Your dad's a writer, isn't he?'

195

Fergus's mum was suddenly breezily bright, a tight smile plastered across her face as if she were presenting a children's TV programme.

Beryl? Little girl? I was liking her less and less by the minute.

'It's Bertie,' Fergus said quietly.

I smiled at him gratefully, but his mum was ignoring us both and chuntering on:

'Don't be shy! Come in and sit down. We've heard *so* much about you from Fenella and that, er, terribly *lively* girl round the corner – Jasmeena, isn't it? She's a character, isn't she? I think I had her full life history in the first five minutes of meeting her.'

I couldn't help feeling a bit sorry for Jazz: it wasn't exactly the most flattering of descriptions. And she *hates* being called by her full name. Wonder how that bit of classified information got out?

'Yeah,' I croaked. Lame or what?

The woman looked at me, her smooth forehead

creased into a mini-frown, but her grin still firmly plastered across her face. 'Oh you *are* shy, aren't you? Honestly, Fergie, you do pick them. For goodness sake go and get Beanie a drink or something. She's your guest.'

'It's Bertie.' I tried correcting her this time.

Fiona Meerley grimaced and said, 'Yes, yes. Charming.'

She pulled Fergus away from the door and down the hall to the kitchen, shouting instructions to him all the way about where to find glasses and squash. Then she half-turned to me and said by way of an explanation: 'We're still in chaos here, I'm afraid. Boxes everywhere!' Gesturing to the sitting room, she said, 'Why don't you wait in there while Fergie gets you a drink?'

Before I could say I didn't want anything, Fiona Meerley had disappeared and was badgering Fergus (sorry, *Fergie*) about something to do with ice cubes and filtered water.

It was weird being in that room again. It certainly looked a lot different from when Pinkella and Kaboodle had lived there. The walls were still pink – I guess the Meerleys wouldn't be allowed to change that kind of thing if they were renting. As for 'boxes everywhere', that was rubbish. Those removal men must have worked like a whole hive of busy bees to get this lot straight. But then, judging by my first impressions of Fiona, she would have been cracking the whip at them all day.

The sitting room was completely tidy in a freaky right-out-of-a-magazine kind of way. Fiona had done an amazing job of working with the pink to produce a mega-modern look that was all sharp edges and glass and metal, and somehow the pink walls actually looked cool. A wave of heat hit me – a mixture of embarrassment and anger. It was bizarre, but I suppose I was feeling put out on Pinkella's behalf. No idea where that came from, as I hadn't exactly been best buddies with her when she'd lived there, and I certainly had not been bowled over by her taste in interior design. But to see someone else move into her place and put their own mark on it, it was — unsettling. Like they'd taken over.

My eyes stopped roaming the walls and I started checking out the furniture. No pink there. Everything was black, grey or white. It made me shiver. I glanced at the floor and realized that the pink fitted carpet had been more or less hidden by a huge white fluffy rug. Oh no! I thought. I bet she's the kind of mum who makes you take your shoes off the minute you walk through the door.

And of course I hadn't, so I'd brought muddy trainer prints in and left a pretty obvious trail on the pristine white rug.

I was just turning round, pondering whether I should take my trainers off and sneak back to the hall to pop them by the door so that I could deny all responsibility for the dark smears on the rug, when a flash of purple caught my eye. Tucked away behind one of the stylish black leather armchairs near the sitting room door was a purple floor cushion. I took a step closer to get a better look at this object which seemed so out of place among all the monochrome. A jolt of electricity went through me. Even though I didn't have anything like it at home, I recognized it immediately from the ones I'd seen in Paws for Thought.

It was a cat bed. A purple cat bed.

14

Catnapped!

'**W**hat are you doing behind the door, Bernie? Here you are — a nice cool drink.' Fiona Meerley had come back in.

I stood up too fast, sending stars spinning into my line of vision. A tall narrow glass of squash, with more ice in it than liquid, had found its way into my hand. It suited Fiona's personality, I thought, as I took it from her. The strong perfume enveloped me again as Fiona stared at the muddy footprints, raising a perfectly plucked eyebrow at me. Something else she and Jazz had in common, that eyebrow . . .

I tried to take a sip of the drink without all the

ice cubes falling on to my face.

'So, are you a keen little dancer like your friend Jasmeena, Barley?' Mrs Meerley asked, sounding as though the very act of talking to me was likely to kill her with boredom.

'Er, it's Bertie,' I said again, rather pointlessly. 'No, I, er, I'm not really into music that much.'

'Oh,' Fiona said archly.

'Where's Fergus?' I blurted out. I was dying to ask him about his cat. Why hadn't he told me he had one?

'He's got some more unpacking to do in his room,' Fiona told me crisply. 'I'm sorry, but I told him he absolutely has to unpack at least three more boxes before he can go out again. I've already promised Jasmeena's mother he would go round there later as it is. She needs him to help her with some of the songs she's practising.'

So much for them not getting on.

'Those two seem to have hit it off right away.

She's very funny, your friend. Did you know her life's ambition is to win *Who's Got Talent?* It's just such a *shame* she's too young to enter this time round,' she said, smiling thinly.

I winced. I knew Jazz was a cringe-makingly awful singer but Fiona was being pretty mean.

Fiona was now prattling on about how her Fergie was *incredibly* musical and what a shame it was about his band splitting up, and how proud she was of him, blah, blah, blah, while I tried to finish the impossibly cold drink as quickly as I could. I had to get out of this room and away from this woman.

'Mrs Meerley,' I began. 'Excuse me for interrupting but—'

At that moment Fergus appeared behind his mum's imposing presence. He peeked out sheepishly at me through his curtain of shiny hair.

Fiona spotted me looking at something over her shoulder and stopped in mid isn't-my-son-wonderful gush. She whirled round sharply and said in a shrill voice: 'Oh, it's you, Fergie dear. You did make me jump! I thought you were unpacking. Oh well, come in and chat to Binky while she finishes her drink, can't you? I've still got a pile of stuff to go through upstairs.' Fiona Meerley stepped to one side to let Fergus through and . . . no, it couldn't be . . . I blinked furiously.

I must have been hallucinating. Surely it wasn't—?

In Fergus's arms, curled up tight and purring like an overheated engine, as orange and fluffy as the day I first set eyes on her, was Jaffa.

I must have looked like a goldfish that's been knocked out of its tank and is limply gasping for air. Fiona's sunny smile had faded to a bewildered creased-up searching look and Fergus had started foot-shuffling. I think it was the foot-shuffling that broke me out of my horrified silence, because Fiona nudged her son at that point and hissed at him not to make 'even more of a mess of the rug', and at the same time I blurted out:

'That's my kitten!'

Great. I sounded like a wheedling toddler who's just had their toy snatched away from them by the playground bully.

Fiona abruptly stopped hissing into Fergus's ear and glanced up sharply, flicking a hank of smoothly preened hair back from her face. She looked suddenly and scarily furious.

'*What* did you say?'

'I – that's my kitten,' I said, stammering. 'Jaffa?' I looked at Jaffa pleadingly, willing her to wriggle out of Fergus's arms and bound up to me.

'Me not Jaffa,' she hissed. 'Me told you that before.'

I gasped, my hand flying to my mouth. Then Fiona laughed. Well, that really did it. 'Yeah,' I said with more feeling. 'She *is* my kitten. She's called Jaffa and I've not had her long. And she's been coming and going and . . . I'd just been talking to

Fergus about it . . .' I tailed off as the most horrible picture began to form in my mind.

Fiona drew back her shoulders. Then she seemed to force herself to relax and plaster on that beaming TV-presenter smile again and her voice softened. 'I'm so sorry to hear that. But this is our kitten; she's called Muffin, not Jaffa. Excuse me, but when *exactly* did you say yours had gone missing?'

'Who missing?' Jaffa mewed. 'Me not missing. Me here.'

I shook my head at her, struck dumb with shock.

'Mum—' Fergus began.

'Shh! I want to hear what Billie has to say,' Fiona said forcefully, but still with that glinting smile.

'Well,' I hesitated. Fiona's response and Jaffa's hurtful behaviour had completely thrown me off course. Not only had I expected Jaffa to fly into my arms, purring with love and affection, I'd also been expecting Fiona to command Fergus to hand

Jaffa over immediately and apologize for a misunderstanding. 'Sh-sh-she's run off a couple of times since we've had her,' I faltered, 'but she's come home in between—'

'Ooooohhh!' Fiona bulldozed in. 'You see, this little one has been here ever since the day we moved in, haven't you, sweetie?' she crooned at Jaffa, leaning over and stroking her luxuriously.

'Yes, me has. And me likes it here. More prawns in this place. And no nasty iron-claw lady,' Jaffa miaowed, pointedly fixing her flashing blue eyes on me.

'She was trying to get into the cat flap the night the removal men arrived, apparently,' Fiona was saying, 'but the landlady had blocked it up when she moved out. We thought this little darling belonged to Ms Pinkington, didn't we, Fergie?' Her shamefaced son nodded through his dark fringe. 'And she seemed so hungry and so lonely. She kept mewing pitifully and looking up at me. I couldn't

ignore her. It was obvious she was simply *starving*.'
She shot me a particularly accusing glance. 'And the
little poppet is so *adorable*. Fergie loves her, don't
you? We *all* love her. Darling Muffin,' she added,
gazing at Jaffa with gooey eyes.

'Everyone loves little old me!'
Jaffa mewed, rubbing her head
against Fergus's arms and purring extra loudly.

Tears were threatening to
spill down my grubby front and an angry
sob was making its way up my throat.

'Hold on a minute,' Fiona said sharply, going
up to Jaffa and running her hand over the kitten's
neck. 'What's happened to that collar I bought her?
Fergus?'

Fergus simply shrugged and avoided my stupe-
fied, tear-filled gaze.

It didn't make sense. It was like one of those
dreams where you find yourself sitting in class in

your pyjamas and everyone else is in uniform. And speaking Chinese. I'd really believed it was Jazz who was the catnapper.

I wanted to grab my naughty kitten and run to Jazz's right away to tell her how sorry I was to have shouted at her and what a fraud this new family was. Once I told her the whole story, she'd soon see what a horrible conniving lot they were, and then she and I would make up and it would be Team Bertie 'n' Jazz again . . .

'Well, I'm very cross,' Fiona was squawking. 'That collar cost a fortune!'

'Mum,' Fergus croaked, 'she's not ours. We can't keep her.'

'What are you talking about?' Fiona snapped.

'Yeah! What the Fergus mewing about?' Jaffa hissed.

'Listen to Bertie,' Fergus persisted, his expression darkening. 'She's just told you how her kitten's been missing – and she told me that Jaffa had come back with a collar on. Face it, Mum, we've made a mistake. Muffin is not a stray. She's already got a home – with Bertie.'

'Fergie!' Fiona said, putting her head on one side and introducing a wheedling tone to her voice. 'I thought you loved this little kitty-cat?'

Fergus scowled dangerously, his deep blue eyes glinting. 'It doesn't matter. She's Bertie's. I'm going to give her back, Mum.'

Thank goodness. I took a step towards Fergus, stretching out a hand to take my kitten back.

Jaffa looked up quizzically, then opened her marble-blue eyes wide and let out an alarmed yowl of surprise.

'Me not going!' she squeaked.

'Jaffa!' I sobbed.

Fiona snorted. 'She doesn't seem to recognize you,' she muttered. Then, taking care to smooth her voice out again, she said silkily, 'Of course we can't keep her, Fergus, *if* she belongs to this young lady.'

Catnapped!

I did not miss the weight Fiona gave to the word 'if'.

I bristled. 'I can prove she's mine—'

'No, no, of course she is. I can see how upset you are. I'm just so sorry that we've caused you alarm,' said Fiona, not sounding sorry at all, in my opinion. 'We wouldn't have fed her if we'd known she belonged to anyone. But, as I said, she looked so *hungry*.' The silky smoothness had developed a raw edge.

What was this woman trying to tell me – that I wasn't responsible enough to look after Jaffa? I could feel my eyes narrowing and my head throbbing with all the things I was desperate to say to this crisply perfect tight-lipped witch of a woman who had *stolen my cat*!

Fiona let out a long sigh and said, 'Give the cat back, Fergie,' as if she were now trying to make out it was all his fault.

He handed Jaffa to me clumsily, mouthing 'sorry'

at me and trying to hold my gaze. But by now I was entirely focused on getting Jaffa home. She was not happy with me, and I received a good couple of scratches and a hiss as I struggled to make her comfortable in the crook of one arm. There was a strong whiff of lemons on her fur, which by now I'd realized must be Fiona's perfume. It was the same scent Jazz had been wearing, I remembered with a twinge of sorrow. The smell made me gag. How was I going to get rid of it?

As I turned to close the front door behind me, Fiona put a hand on my shoulder. Letting her head drop to one side and fixing her eyes on Jaffa, she said in a voice dripping with care and concern, 'We will miss the dear little thing. She'd become quite a feature in our new home. We really are rather smitten with her. You know . . .' She paused. 'I'm not sure I'll be able to resist feeding her again if she comes round looking so *ravenously* hungry.'

I bit my lip so hard I could taste blood in my

mouth, and forcing a sour smile said, 'I'll make sure that doesn't happen.'

I hurried across the road without looking back, clutching Jaffa to me so tightly she began to scramble to try and free herself.

'No chance,' I said, keeping my voice low so that the Meerleys wouldn't be able to hear me. 'You are coming home. With me.'

213

15

A Light-bulb Moment

I've no idea how I managed to escape from the Meerleys' without committing the sort of crime that would have had me thrown behind bars for the rest of my life. All I know is that I did get back over the road to my house without dropping the snarling, spitting bundle that was Jaffa.

I wrestled with trying to open the door and holding on to Jaffa and quickly realized it would be easier to ring the bell, even though I knew it would probably annoy Dad. I braced myself for a why-don't-you-take-your-own-keys-instead-of-disturbing-me rant, but instead, Dad looked flustered and hassled when he answered.

A Light-bulb Moment

'Oh!' he cried, his eyes on stalks as he noticed Jaffa. 'Thank goodness you've got her!' He enveloped us in a huge bear hug, with Jaffa between us like a fluffy, squeaking sandwich filling. 'I thought she'd gone again,' he babbled, releasing us from his grip.

'Me *had* gone,' Jaffa mewed. 'And me is going again after that icky-squishy squash-hug.'

'No you don't,' I said in a low voice.

'What's that?' Dad asked, peering at me oddly.

'I said, "Yes, she had" – gone again, that is,' I said, thinking on my feet.

Dad frowned. 'You didn't take her out with you? I wish you'd told me. I've been worried sick.'

'No, no. Listen, Dad, you won't believe what that horrible woman over the road has been up to—'

'Prawn lady not horrible!' Jaffa protested.

'She IS!' I hissed into her ear.

'Bertie.' Dad cut in on what was threatening to turn into a full-scale three-way argument of worry-ingly complicated proportions. I looked up from my kitten to see him staring over my shoulder at something. 'I think you'll have to save that story for later.'

I whirled round and came face to face with Fergus.

'It's the Fergus!' Jaffa mewed excitedly and wriggled harder than ever.

I pushed Dad aside and marched purposefully into the house. How dare he follow me home after what his mum had just done!

I heard Dad say, 'Hello!' and Fergus mutter, 'Hi.' Then Dad called after me, 'Hey, Bertie. Come back, please. You've got a visitor.' He made it quite clear from his tone of voice how rude I was being. I turned back slowly, still keeping a firm grip on Jaffa.

'What do you want?' I spluttered at Fergus.

'Bertie . . .' Dad said slowly, frowning over the top of his glasses to admonish me, just like he's done ever since I was a baby. But it wasn't going to work this time.

216

A Light-bulb Moment

'I don't know what you think you're doing, coming here—' I shouted.

'I came to say sorry!' Fergus shouted back.

I jumped.

'Ow! Bertie hurted Jaffsie!' Jaffa protested, as I squashed her into my chest.

'Well, stay still then,' I muttered as quietly as I could.

'Bertie, I think you need to calm down,' Dad said.

'Yeah, you should be nice to the Fergus. He coooool,' Jaffa purred.

'Shut up!' It slipped out . . .

'BERTIE!'

'It's all right,' Fergus said, reddening as he held up one hand to stop us. 'Listen, I feel really bad about this, Bertie.'

'No, you don't!' I snapped. 'You *knew* how upset

I was about Jaffa — I told you all about it the first time we met. Now I suppose you're going to tell me that she came round and absolutely *begged* to be let into your place and that you couldn't help feeding her because she looked so hungry and saaaaad—' I pulled a face and put on a sing-song voice, mimicking his mum.

'Oh, Bertie!' Dad admonished. He looked angry and ashamed. Ashamed of me, I realized with a sting. 'That's no way to talk. I've no idea what's been going on between you two . . . Goodness knows I've no idea what goes on most of the time these days, Bertie. First you and Jazz and now this—'

'Dad. Do you think you could leave us alone for a moment? Please?' I added, struggling to keep my Tone of Voice under control. Dad screwed his mouth tight shut and looked for a moment as though he was tussling with the idea of shouting me down and locking me up for a month. But by some miracle, he decided to back off.

A Light-bulb Moment

'OK,' he said calmly. 'But I'll be upstairs if you need me.'

Yeah, and listening in, no doubt, I thought grimly.

'Come into the kitchen,' I grunted to Fergus. Our house was the mirror image of Pinkella's so he knew where to go, but I led the way anyway.

'Is Jaffsie getting a yummy treat?' my kitten purred. She looked up at me with her melty eyes.

'Didn't you already get something to eat?' I snapped.

'What?' Fergus said, puzzled.

'Oh, nothing,' I said, too irritable to be embarrassed. I plonked myself down on a chair and Jaffa actually settled on my lap, I was relieved to see. 'So?' I said, staring at Fergus challengingly.

Fergus looked appalled. 'Hey, I'm really sorry you're so upset about this. But it's not me you should be mad at — it's Mum. She's nuts about cats.' He shrugged. 'We all are: me, Mum *and* Dad really. We used to have one — but that's another story. I don't think you'd be interested. And I know it's no excuse, but you have to admit your kitten is pretty adorable.'

'I *know* she is!' I spluttered.

'You is sooooo right,' Jaffa added, stretching out her front paws.

I ignored her. The cute act was not working. I was livid. 'So. What I don't get is, why did you let me go on and on about how I thought it was *Jazz* who was enticing Jaffa away when all the time it was your mum? You've made me look stupid.'

'I don't think you look stupid,' Fergus said quietly.

I closed my eyes. He was not going to stop me being angry with him, no matter what he said. 'And you knew I'd fallen out with Jazz too. Everything's gone wrong!' I almost howled that last bit.

'I'm sorry . . .' Fergus muttered.

I opened my eyes and narrowed them at Fergus in a scowl. '*Why didn't you tell me?*' I insisted.

A Light-bulb Moment

He sighed deeply and looked around the room, as if he was searching for inspiration. 'I honestly don't know. To start with I genuinely didn't put two and two together – when we first met, I mean. I just thought it was a bit of a coincidence. Then when I did realize Muffin – I, I mean Jaffa – was your cat, it was kind of too late to admit it.'

'What do you mean, too late?' I snapped.

'Why Bertie so cross with the Fergus?' Jaffa whined.

'Because he's an idiot,' I hissed under my breath.

'Listen, I should go,' Fergus said, pushing back his chair.

'No, you haven't explained properly,' I said grumpily.

Fergus's eyes were wide and panicky. He looked a bit like a rabbit caught in the headlights of oncoming traffic. 'I just meant . . . I just meant that I really like you and I didn't want you to hate me.' It came out in such a rush I wasn't sure I'd heard him correctly.

'Me like you too,' Jaffa said softly. 'Me like Bertie *and* the Fergus.'

My head was spinning. I'd lurched from upset to fury to embarrassment in under a minute. I put out a hand to hold on to the edge of the table.

Fergus hurried on: 'Once I'd worked it out, I told Mum you'd be angry. I crept over to yours and brought Jaffa back, but she kept following me home. And when I told Mum I thought it was getting ridiculous, she just said she couldn't help it if your cat liked coming over to our place.'

'Everybody love Jaffsie!' Jaffa crooned.

'Yeah, a bit too much,' I muttered. Then to Fergus: 'Why doesn't your mum get her own cat, then?'

Fergus nodded, lowering his eyes. 'I know. I told her that. She said she and Dad had discussed it but it wouldn't work cos they both have to move around with their jobs so much. Bertie, I've tried everything to get my parents to let me have a pet – you have no idea.' Actually, I do, I thought grimly. 'I gave up on the cat idea long ago, but Mum won't even let me have a rabbit or a guinea pig. She says it's too much of a tie, especially if we're only staying here for a couple of months . . .' He tailed off and fixed me with a crestfallen look from those dark blue eyes.

Only a couple of months?

'S-so,' I stammered. I was intrigued that Fergus seemed as animal-mad as me, but I couldn't let myself get distracted. 'What was your mum planning to do with Jaffa the next time you all went away, then?'

Fergus shrugged again. 'I don't think she thinks of herself as Muf— Jaffa's owner as such,' he said. 'I suppose she thought Jaffa would come home to you when she wasn't at our place.'

'Fabby-dooby idea!' Jaffa agreed.

'Rubbish idea!' I snapped. 'Your – I mean, Jaffa's – home is *here* and that means one hundred per cent of the time, not just every other day or week or whatever,' I said. This conversation was getting pretty confusing.

Fergus was looking more and more out of his depth. 'Listen, I'd really better be getting back. I am seriously sorry about all this. Like I said, I told Mum you'd be angry. Hey, if there's anything I can do to make it up to you? Anything at all. I just feel so bad . . .' He had got up from the table and shoved his hands into his pockets. He looked like a naughty puppy who's just been told off for raiding the fridge. In spite of everything I felt myself softening.

'No,' I shot back at him, forcing myself to put all my energy into staying angry. 'You've done enough— '

I stopped.

Would he really do 'anything' to help? I wondered. Even if it meant helping me sort things out with Jazz?

I had had one of those rare and blinding brain-flash ideas that Dad calls 'light-bulb moments', like the time I'd been doodling on a piece of paper and come up with the idea for my Pet-Sitting Service. Boy, did that feel like a lifetime ago!

'Er, you were saying?' Fergus prompted me nervously.

I pulled myself together, aware that I had one finger in mid-air, and was staring into the middle distance like a mad professor who's just found the cure for insanity but can't quite apply it to himself.

'Huh?' I said.

'You were saying something and then you stopped,' Fergus said, looking at me strangely.

'Yes, you – er – you asked if there was anything you could do. Well, I've just realized there *is* something, actually . . .'

And I proceeded to lay out my request to Fergus Meerley. A request that would make up for all the hassle with Jaffa, and one that would hopefully mend my friendship with Jazz and put her in my debt for months – if not years – to come.

16

Friends Again

Fergus had been as reluctant as a dog at bath time when I outlined my plan, but he was in a tight corner since saying he'd do 'anything' to make things up to me.

'And you've got to promise not to mention any of this to Jazz until we've got an agreement with your mum,' I told him as he made his way to the door.

He turned to me anxiously, his hand on the doorknob. 'Bertie, Jazz isn't talking to me at the moment. I told you that. And I'm really not sure that Mum will—'

I wasn't interested in these details. 'Fergus, you

said you wanted to help,' I said, my voice dripping (I hoped) with menace.

'Yeah, yeah, OK,' Fergus said, flustered. 'I'll – er, I'll see what I can do. I definitely need to talk to Mum first. I'll come back round later and let you know what she's said.'

'I'll be waiting,' I replied.

He hovered, showing no signs of making a move.

I raised one eyebrow. 'So? What are you waiting for?'

Fergus left.

Dad came down a split second later. I knew he'd been listening.

'You've got that boy where you want him, haven't you?' Dad teased.

'Yeah, Bertie likes the Fergus!' Jaffa purred.

I flushed. 'What do you mean?'

'Looks to me like he'd do anything for you!' Dad winked.

227

'Bertie in luuuurve!' Jaffa crooned.

'Doh!' I huffed at them both and flounced off with Jaffa, turning my back pointedly on Dad.

'Listen, Jaffsie,' I whispered in her ear as I took her into the sitting room for a private chat. 'Please just sit tight with me and wait for Fergus to come back with the news. I really need him to help me if Jazz and I are ever going to be mates again.'

'OK,' Jaffa said, and rolled on her back on my lap, offering herself up for a tummy tickle.

I sighed. How could I feel so irritated with her one minute and so gooey inside the next? If Kaboodle and this little kitten were anything to go by, I'd say cats were pretty tricky customers, I thought to myself. Almost as tricky as best friends.

★

Friends Again

Fergus came round about an hour later with his mother in tow. Dad had gone out, thank goodness; I couldn't have handled any more of his nudge-nudge-wink-winking.

I asked Fergus and Fiona into the sitting room while I fantasized about wrapping my hands around the woman's throat and yelling 'CATNAPPER!' into her face. But then I thought that probably wouldn't help me win Jazz back with my cunning plan, so I sat down with Jaffa on my lap and kept quiet while Fiona spoke.

'So, Beanie,' she said.

'Mum, for the millionth time, it's Bertie,' Fergus said in exasperation. He waited for his mum to say something else (like, maybe apologize?) but she just stared at him with her arms crossed. He rolled his eyes and said, 'Mum's just been saying how sorry we were about encouraging Jaffa,' Fiona opened and shut her mouth like an appalled goldfish but Fergus ploughed on bravely, 'and I suggested we do something to make it up to you.'

'The Fergus telling porky pies!' Jaffa squeaked. '*Bertie* said that, not the Fergus!'

'Shh, Jaffa,' I whispered. 'It doesn't matter.'

'Muffin – sorry, *Jaffa* – seems a little upset. Is she all right?' Fiona cooed.

'*Mum!*' Fergus protested. His voice had an edge to it now that even Fiona seemed to notice. She fell silent and gestured to him to continue. He looked at me and took a deep breath. 'You and I both know how much Jazz wants an audition for *Who's Got Talent?*—'

'Lovely girl, that Jasmeena,' Fiona interrupted. 'And of course in any other circumstances I'd be *delighted* to help her in any way I could. But the thing is, my hands are tied on this one.'

I stared at her blankly.

'It's like I've already said. The rules,' Fergus said bluntly, looking awkward.

'Jasmeena knows she has to be sixteen to enter,' Fiona added.

'Mum,' Fergus said. He looked pleadingly at her, but I could tell they had already been over this one a few thousand times back at their place.

'Darling,' Fiona said firmly, 'I told you. And I'm telling Bunty here: I simply *can't* change the rules. I'm only the producer. These rules are written and decided on way in advance of filming and there are all sorts of regulations to do with allowing minors to compete in things like this. Now, I was going to take you into town this morning, wasn't I, Fergie? And I'm sure Bunny here is incredibly busy too, so now we've explained everything, let's say goodbye, shall we?'

I was glaring at Fergus, willing him to stand up to his mum, but he was completely deflated and just nodded weakly at Fiona.

Jaffa chose this moment to kick up a right racket. 'What the lady talking 'bout? Tell me, Bertie! Tell meeeeee!'

'Shh! I'll tell you later,' I whispered into her small

231

pink ear, hoping no one would hear me above the noise she was making.

'Noooo! Me wants to know nooooow!' she miaowed, wriggling to get free of my grasp.

'It's just a competition thing – for people,' I hissed. I was aware that Fiona and Fergus were gawping at me as though I was a one-woman freak show, but I had to try and calm Jaffa down. She was struggling harder now and I was fighting to keep hold of her as she scratched and clawed her way out of my grasp.

'Me want be in competition!' she miaowed. 'Me want win prizes!'

'No, Jaffa, it's not a pet show,' I said, struggling to keep my voice low. 'Be quiet now.'

'A pet show?' Fergus said, puzzled. 'What are you talking about?'

Jaffa nipped me and, with a gasp, I dropped her. She shot me a look of glee and said, 'Can't catch Jaffsie!' and went trotting over to Fiona and jumped on her lap.

I stared open-mouthed.

'*This* lady knows me can win prizes,' Jaffa purred, rubbing her head on Fiona's hand.

Fiona's face softened. 'Aaaah! Hello, little baby,' she said in a sing-song voice. 'You really are the most *beautiful* little kitten, aren't you, sweetie? You would win a talent show any day, wouldn't you? Yes, you would. You would win all the prizes.' She cooed and petted and went on and on like this for several seconds. I glared at Fergus, venom oozing from my eyes.

But instead of Fergus looking away in shame, or pulling his mum up and telling her she had to go, or any other suitably contrite reaction I was hoping for, his velvety blue eyes grew larger and larger, his jaw dropped lower and lower and then, drowning out his mother's pathetic baby-talk, he leaped to his feet and yelled:

'PET SHOW!'

233

'Yeeeeooow!' yelped Jaffa, sinking her claws into Fiona's pristine purple skirt.

'DARLING!' Fiona yelled, leap-ing to her feet and knocking Jaffa flying.

Jaffa landed in a heap and looked up at me pitifully. 'Lady dropped Jaffsie!' she mewled.

But I'd hardly noticed. Because I'd just had my second light-bulb moment of the day, and I had a strong suspicion it was the same one as Fergus's.

Fiona was brushing furiously at her skirt and mut-tering, 'Whatever is the matter with you two?'

'Pet show, Mum!' Fergus repeated, his face shin-ing with excitement. 'Just think – you could tie it in with *Who's Got Tal—*'

'Darlings!' Fiona cut in, her eyes lighting up. 'I've just had the most marvellous idea: we could put on a pet show to run alongside *Who's Got Talent?!*'

I raised my eyebrows at Fergus.

DRIIIING!

Great! What now?

I went to the door.

'Hi! Thought I'd come round and see if you were still alive . . .'

Jazz? Oh no, why did she have to choose this precise moment in time to break our war of silence?

She bounced into the sitting room. But her bounciness came to an abrupt halt when she saw Fergus and Fiona. She curled her lip at Fergus. 'What are *you* doing here?' she demanded.

'Hi, Jazz,' I said quietly.

Why can't she just ask me how I am for a change? I thought. I had a sudden picture of the two of us hugging and saying sorry to each other and walking back to her place arm in arm, just like we would have done before the Miserable Meerleys appeared on the scene. No Meerleys, no talent auditions, no disappearing cat act . . .

Fergus was staring at the carpet, looking as though the end of the world could not come soon enough.

'Hello, Jasmeena!' Fiona trilled. 'You've arrived just in time to hear my brilliant idea!' she announced.

She really was unbelievable. How that woman had managed to give birth to someone as nice as Fergus . . . I stopped that thought double-quick before a full-on infra-red blush melted my face into smithereens.

'Right,' Jazz said, sneering. 'And what's your brilliant idea got to do with me?'

Incredibly, Fiona didn't seem to have picked up on Jazz's icy tone of voice. She smiled a wide, pleased-with-herself smile and almost purred, 'We've been talking about *Who's Got Talent?*, Jasmeena dear.' Jazz's face immediately lit up like the Eiffel Tower at night. 'And how it's such a shame you're not old enough for the auditions,' Fiona continued. All the lights went out again in Jazz's face and it plummeted into a ferocious grimace of disgust. (I couldn't help being impressed by the way Fiona motored over Jazz, not giving her a chance to say a word. I never thought I'd see Jasmeena Brown meet her match.) 'I'm sorry to be brutal about it, Jasmeena dear, but the rules are the rules and I did not write them. *But*,' she paused dramatically and the atmosphere in the room crackled with expectation, 'I think I might just have come up with something else that could take your fancy.'

'Oh . . . yeah?' Jazz croaked.

She was completely at sea. She didn't know whether to smile or scowl. As for me, until I'd heard the whole deal, I was definitely not going to get excited. What if Fiona was going to suggest we dress up as chickens? Or did she have a box of fluffy bunny costumes upstairs that we would have to wear around town? I always felt so sorry for those people, especially in this summer's heat.

Mind you, I had a sneaking suspicion that Jazz would do anything to get her fifteen minutes of fame.

'And it's all down to this lovely little cat here,' Fiona went on, stroking Jaffa's ears.

'Me is pretty clever that way,' Jaffa purred, washing her paws diligently. She looked up at me and flashed her blue eyes as if she was winking. 'And me knows how to make *everybody* happy . . .' she added.

'So?' Jazz asked. 'What *is* the big idea?'

Fiona gave a twinkling laugh. 'A talent show for pets! We could run it in the early slot before *Who's Got Talent?* and we could ask members of the public to enter their pets and then the viewers at home would be able to ring in and vote. We can call it *Pets With Talent!* and the proceeds from the voting could go to the Cats and Dogs Home. That would be sure to get us publicity.' She was on a roll now.

'There could be categories for cutest pet – which darling Muff— Jaffa would be sure to win . . .' she simpered.

'What did me tell you?' Jaffa purred.

' . . . and then there would be fastest pet, cleverest pet – the possibilities are endless!' Fiona breathed, clapping her hands together.

'Great,' said Jazz sourly. 'So where exactly do I fit into this?'

Fiona had blown it. Pets were not the way to Jazz's heart.

Fergus coughed and said, 'Yeah, Mum – this isn't really Jazz's thing.'

My eyes darted to the floor. Could that boy read my mind?

Fiona laughed that sparkly laugh again. 'Ah, but this is where the best bit comes – we get *celebrities* to be the judges! In fact, I think Simon and Danni would LOVE this. It would bring a whole new angle to the existing TV programme, and they both have pets they're *crazy* about, so they're bound to say yes. Fergie, darling, I'm going to get on the phone to them right away,' she said, already halfway out of the room.

'Hold it,' Jazz said sternly. I had to admire the nerve of the girl, talking to Fiona like that. 'I still don't get this,' she said. 'It's OK for Bertie – she can enter Jaffa. But what about me? I don't have any pets.'

'You have Huckleberry,' Fergus pointed out, meekly.

'That rat's not *mine!*' Jazz cried, flinging her hands in the air in horror.

Fiona turned back to Jazz and laid a perfectly manicured hand on her shoulder. 'But darling, you would be the most important person in all of this,' she said soothingly. 'Danni and Simon would need a personal assistant to show them around and introduce them to all the contestants. And I think you would be utterly perfect for the job. And who knows, they might be persuaded to have a little chat with you about, how shall I put it . . . your future career opportunities?'

Jazz's face went through every possible emotion in the space of a minute: from disgust to shock to disbelief to out-and-out sheer and totally hysterical joy.

'Woooooo!' she shouted, throwing her arms around Fiona. 'Thank you!' she cried.

Fiona disentangled herself and patted Jazz firmly on the arm. 'Actually, it's not me you should thank.' She looked at me and Fergus pointedly.

Jazz turned to look at us too and frowned. 'Eh?'

Fiona sighed. 'Fergus told me that Barnie wanted to try and get you an audition – against all the odds, I might add. If he hadn't come to talk to me about that, and if I'd never met that gorgeous little kitten, I never would have thought of the pet show.'

'Is this true?' Jazz whispered hoarsely.

Fergus nodded silently.

Jazz gawped at us.

'So, can we be friends again?' My mouth blurted it out before my brain had a chance to put the brakes on.

'Oh, Bertie. I'm sorry.' Jazz ran and threw her arms around me. I felt a tidal wave of relief engulf me. 'I've been a total numpty,' she mumbled into my shoulder. 'I was so cross, I didn't know what I was saying the other day. Forgive me? I have missed you, you know.'

'Me too,' I admitted.

We drew back from each other's embrace and grinned sheepishly.

Fergus was smiling at us shyly. Without thinking I rushed at him and crushed him in a bear hug. 'THANK YOU!' I yelled.

'Hey!' Jazz sounded mildly indignant. I peeled myself away from Fergus, struggling hard to keep my personal temperature gauge at 'normal'. I grimaced as if to say, 'Don't know what came over me there!' but I needn't have worried, as Jazz then hurled herself at Fergus and squeezed the life out of him too.

Dad came home in the middle of it all, and soon Jazz and Fiona were both filling him in on the plans in high-pitched excitable voices.

'Is Bertie pleased with Jaffsie?' my kitten mewed, coming be-tween me and the others.

I bent down to stroke her, and taking advantage of all the noise and mayhem surrounding me said, 'You bet, little Jaffa Cake. You bet.'

The Dream Team was back together and we were unstoppable.

17

All Systems Go

Jazz was the most hyper I had ever seen her. And that is saying something about the girl who whoops and screams at most things in life like a monkey who's got the best banana. Still, she might have been bouncing like a kangaroo on hot tarmac but, boy, it was good to have my best mate around again!

'I can't belieeeeeeve it!' she said for the millionth time that day. 'I'm going to meet Simon – and Danni! I think I'm going to dieeee! This is real, isn't it? Pinch me, Bertie, so I know it's real!'

I chuckled. Jazz was already referring to the celebrity *WGT?* judges by their first names, even though we were a long way off being introduced.

'What are they like?' she quizzed Fergus. The three of us were round at my place just as we'd been every day for the past week, planning the pet show, brainstorming ideas, and making endless lists of the kind of animals we'd like to enter.

Fergus shrugged and drew a doodle on a piece of paper. 'I dunno. Simon's like he is on the telly – grumpy and rude. Danni's – er . . . well, she's pretty, I guess. Not as pretty as some people, though,' he said, shooting me a shy smile.

I made a big deal out of scribbling hard on my notepad so that Jazz wouldn't see me blush.

But Jazz wouldn't have noticed if Fergus had jumped up and snogged me there and then: she had her sights set on far starrier things. 'I bet Simon's a real pussycat once you get to know him,' she simpered, staring at the ceiling, her hands clasped together like some lame Disney princess. 'I'm going to make sure I get a chance to sing to him.' And she broke into a screechy version of her favourite song of the moment.

'Oh no! Make the Jazzer stop!' Jaffa mewled in horror from the beanbag where she'd been snoozing. 'Her singing badder even than Uncle Kaboodle's.'

I sniggered behind my hand.

'What're you laughing at?' Jazz spat, whirling on me.

'Hey, so how're we doing with the list of people we're going to ask?' Fergus jumped in.

He'd been like this ever since Jazz and I had made up, acting the go-between at the slightest sign of trouble.

'Oh, right. Let's see . . . Bertie, you were going to talk to Mr Smythe?' Jazz immediately seemed to forget what she'd been cross about and shook her papers authoritatively.

Fergus had an amazingly soothing effect on Jazz now that her dream was on the verge of coming true. I grinned at him gratefully, making a mental note to be more careful how I reacted to my kitten's interjections. I did not want to run the risk of falling out with Jazz like that again. Ever.

While Fiona went into action with Simon Cow and Danni Minnow and all the telly people, Jazz, Fergus and I got busy recruiting pets for the show. Fiona had said she had many contacts who would help her find willing contestants, 'Although it would be rather sweet to involve a few friends and neighbours,' she added.

I went to see Mr Smythe first of all. He had been my only other customer when I was running my Pet-Sitting Service, so I felt I owed it to him to ask if he wanted to enter his hamsters.

He was thrilled, twitching his little nose, fiddling with his moustache, his eyes crinkling in delight.

'My, my! I say, what a terrific idea. Just wait till I tell the little chaps about this!' he twittered. 'Perhaps they could be persuaded to do some tricks for

247

the cameras? Mr Nibbles has developed the most remarkable gift of being able to cram quite an astounding number of sunflower seeds into his pouches at any one time. And as for Houdini – well, his gift of escapology needs to be seen to be believed.'

I swallowed hard and tried not to react to this last bit – I remembered Houdini's escape act far too well. The last time I'd found him out of his cage he had been lucky not to end up as a hamster sandwich for dear old Kaboodle.

'I – er – I'm not sure we could cope with escaping hamsters in front of the TV cameras,' I said hesitantly. 'Especially with other larger animals around.'

Mr Smythe chuckled in that dry, high-pitched way of his and blinked hard at me. 'You are a funny girl, Roberta,' he said. 'I won't let Houdini out of the *cage* – don't worry. He can do his tricks *in* the cage, escaping from an old loo roll or margarine box – that kind of thing.'

I smiled stiffly. I could just imagine Fiona's reaction to this idea . . . The man really was a loop-the-loop fruit-loop loony. 'Sounds fun,' I said and quickly made my excuses.

When I told Fergus and Jazz about Mr Smythe later that week, Fergus roared with laughter. 'Man! He sounds bonkers! That's just the kind of thing that makes good telly, though. Bertie, you're a genius.'

Jazz bristled. 'Yeah, well, I just think he's weird. OK, who's next?'

'Mr Bruce?' I suggested. 'He's got those two King Charles spaniels.'

'Oh. My. Goodness,' Jazz breathed, her hands flung up in mock horror. 'You cannot *seriously* be thinking of letting that muppet enter with those Hounds of the Basketcase, can you?'

I shrugged. 'Might liven things up a bit,' I said weakly.

Fergus chuckled. 'Cool!' he said. 'Let's go and see him right away.'

249

As we walked up to Mr Bruce's front door, I felt suddenly sick with nerves. What if he slammed the door in my face? So far the only animals I had definitely managed to round up for Fergus and his mum were Jaffa, the hamsters, Huckleberry and Sparky from the pet shop. (I had swallowed my pride and asked Dad to call 'Bex'. Unsurprisingly, he'd been thrilled about that.)

The second my hand touched the doorbell a riot of barking and scrabbling paws rocketed towards the front door. I took a nervous step back as I heard footsteps and a man's deep voice saying, 'Down, Digby! Down, Buzz!'

Jazz rolled her eyes and stuck out one hip, shooting me a withering I-told-you-so look.

Fergus grimaced and held up crossed fingers.

The door opened slightly as Mr Bruce tried to restrain his two over-eager dogs.

'Be with you in a minute!' he shouted over the noise. 'Down, boys!' he yelled at the dogs, then opened the door a fraction more. 'Just let me get these two on leads,' he said, peering out at me. He let the door swing to and was back in an instant, having clipped leads to the spaniels' collars. When he opened the door properly I noticed he looked rather hot and bothered. His forehead was shiny with sweat and he was a bit out of breath.

'Sorry about that,' he grunted, yanking back sharply on the leads to prevent the dogs from pulling him over. 'Always get overexcited when the bell goes. Must train it out of them,' he muttered. Then he seemed to remember that I hadn't said hello or anything yet and beamed at me, showing a set of rather vicious-looking teeth.

'Ah, Roberta and Jasmeena,' he said.

Jazz let out a loud sigh.

I frowned at her and said, 'Yeah. Well, Bertie and Jazz actually.'

'And—?' he asked, nodding at Fergus.

I introduced him and was about to launch into

an explanation of why we'd come round when Mr Bruce cut in abruptly. 'Very well, very well—Heeeeeeel!' he barked, yanking his dogs' leads fiercely.

The spaniels were straining harder than ever on their leads, practically choking themselves in their effort to get closer to me. I tried to take a good look at them, but they were panting and jumping and pulling so much all I really took in was two long pink tongues and a lot of gross slobbery stuff coming out of the corners of their mouths.

Jazz had started muttering about having a lot to do and turned to leave, but Fergus restrained her and nodded at me encouragingly.

'Er, how old are your dogs?' I asked.

'Only two,' Mr Bruce said. 'Bouncy brutes, aren't they?' He seemed very pleased with this comment, and gave a wheezy laugh.

'Right. Well, the reason I'm here is that we're organizing a pet show, but . . .' I hesitated. 'Erm,

I'm not sure that you'd be interested actually,' I said hastily, suddenly making up my mind that this was not a good idea, and backing away from the two slavering beasts. But Mr Bruce had caught sight of one of the posters that Fergus was carrying and he started reading it, peering through his glasses awkwardly while still pulling hard on the dog leads.

'Oh, my two boys will love this!' he cried, when he'd finished reading.

'I didn't know you had children,' I said, puzzled.

Mr Bruce squinted at me and then let out another creaky chuckle. 'I meant these boys!' he said, gesturing to the dogs. 'It's just the thing they need actually – bit of an incentive to work harder on the training. Could do a little agility display for you, eh?'

I grabbed the poster from Fergus and mumbled something about leaving him time to think about it. Then quickly making our excuses, we ran off.

Fergus and I were barely able to wait until we'd reached the corner before a fit of hiccuppy giggles overtook us.

'Oh, my two little fellas are simply spiffing!' Fergus squawked, in an exaggerated impression of Mr Bruce.

'Yes, yes, all tip-top and shipshape!' I howled.

'What is he *like*?' Fergus cried, clutching his stomach and whooping as he tried to get his breath back.

Jazz was seriously unamused. 'When you two have finished behaving like a couple of nursery school kids, perhaps we could get on with finding some more *suitable* entrants for this competition?' she said scathingly, wobbling her head at us.

That shut me up. I gulped, realizing the truth of what Jazz had just said. Mr Bruce was a loser, Mr Smythe was a nutcase . . . How had I ever believed this was going to work? I was silent all the way home, wondering what mayhem I had unleashed.

18

Kitten's Got Talent!

The show came round far too quickly. A crippling sensation of unease seized me whenever I thought about it. The way things had been going for me recently, I was convinced the whole thing had 'MASSIVE DISASTER AREA' written all over it in ten-foot-high capital letters. Even Fergus's repeated assurances that it would all be 'all right on the night' were doing nothing to steady my nerves.

'Thing is,' I told him the day before the show, 'if it all goes wrong, it's going to be my fault.'

He shook his head at me affectionately, his russet fringe flopping over his face. 'Don't be so down on yourself, Bertie. It's going to be brilliant. Mum will make sure it runs like clockwork, Jazz will keep Simon and Danni happy just by being there and loving everything they say and do, and you and I – ' he glanced away, running his hand through his hair and grinning – 'we'll keep the animals under control. We're a great team,' he added bashfully.

That night, Jaffa jumped up on to my bed and curled into the crook of my arm. She fell into a

deep sleep immediately, whereas I could not settle at all. No matter what Fergus said, my stomach was churning and my mind was torturing me with images of Mr Bruce's dogs trying to eat Huckleberry, or the hamsters, or Jaffa – or all three.

At least we'd got a few more entrants together. Dad had proudly told me 'Bex' had come up with a list of twenty other customers who she thought would bring their pets along, so altogether it looked as though we had twenty-five entrants to tell Fiona about, including Sparky and Jaffa. At least something good had come out of Dad batting his eyelashes at that woman, I thought with a sigh.

I hoped Fiona had been able to get more entrants through her contacts. She hadn't been very communicative. And I wasn't sure that in reality Simon Cow and Danni Minnow were going to be the slightest bit interested either. Who was I kidding? They were coming to our town for the *WGT?* auditions, not some schoolgirl's pet show.

I tossed and turned while my kitten snuffled softly on my duvet.

'Jaffa?' I whispered. 'Can I talk to you?'

The tiny kitten snuffled in her sleep and put her paw over her face. My chest tightened at the sight of her. Whatever else happened, at least I had my Jaffa. She hadn't run off at all since we'd started planning the pet show. She seemed completely at home with me. And she had totally stolen my heart.

'Jaffsie?' I tried again.

'Mmmm?' she purred, opening one eye cautiously, and then stretched and yawned. 'Me sleeping,' she said grumpily.

'I know,' I said, stroking her downy fur, 'but I can't sleep at all tonight.'

'Well, me is very sorry. But me *can* sleep and me going right back to sleep, right now!' Jaffa said, closing her eyes firmly.

'Hey! Just a minute!' I said, picking her up and putting her on my chest so that her face was close to mine. 'I just want to ask you something about tomorrow.'

'Tomorrow is tomorrow. Mum said,' Jaffa said huffily. 'And today is today. And right now me is sleepy. Me *told* Bertie this!'

'OK!' I said impatiently. 'Just one minute of your time – that's all I'm asking.'

Jaffa sighed noisily, opened one eye and said,

'One minute.'

I tickled her gently behind one ear. 'Thank you. So, I wanted to say, are you nervous about the pet show?'

Jaffa blinked slowly. 'Nervous? Why should *me* be nervous?'

'Well, it's a sort of competition, the pet show. Sometimes people get nervous before competitions. And there'll be other animals there that maybe you've never seen before. I just wondered if you'd thought about it.'

'Everyone always loves Jaffsie,' she said. I'm sure she smiled as she said this. Cheeky little monkey! I thought. I wish I had her confidence. 'So me is not worried about nothin'. And,' she said, opening her eyes wide and fixing me with that innocent gaze of hers, 'if my Bertie there to look after Jaffsie, there be nothin' to worry about anyway.'

My heart lurched. 'That's right, little Jaffa,' I whispered. 'That's right.'

259

Kitten Wars

★

It turned out that both Fergus and my little kitten were completely one hundred per cent right: there was nothing to worry about. I had not taken Fergus at his word when he'd said his mum would run everything like clockwork – it was more like a military parade, if you asked me. That woman was as efficient as a whole army of ants. Fiona had sorted the venue (the Pinkington Theatre which Dad and Pinkella had helped to renovate, and where the *Who's Got Talent?* auditions were also to be held). She had also organized all the other contestants and of course the TV crews and make-up people and the catering people who were needed to provide refreshments and snacks.

The only thing Fiona couldn't control was Jazz. If I'd thought my best mate had been hyper during the planning of this thing, her behaviour on the morning of the show was mega-ultra-super-hyper! She was like a jitter-bug with a sugar rush.

She could not keep still, patting her hair, rearranging her bangles on her arm, pulling at her T-shirt, and squealing every time she caught sight of a TV camera or a microphone.

'You need to chill out, Jazz,' Fergus told her. 'Just be yourself. Danni and Simon are going to love you. Mum's told them so much about you.'

'Oh yeah, like what a freak I am and how I'm only eleven and—' her face darkened as she realized she'd given away her real age.

Fergus raised an eyebrow at me and smiled knowingly.

'Fergus is right, Jazz,' I said, grabbing my funny friend and hugging her tight. 'They'll love you – just like we do.'

Of course they did! And weirdly, they seemed to love me too, which I was pretty surprised about. They weren't nearly as diva-like as I'd thought they would be. Even Simon was brilliant at chatting to us, joking and laughing and putting us

261

completely at our ease. Danni even let us look around their mega black limo, which had a DVD player and a fridge stacked with chocolate and drinks. I could certainly see why the celebrity life appealed to Jazz.

'Can't go anywhere without my candy bars!' Danni drawled, offering us each a snack from the fridge. 'Take a note of that, chick.' She winked at Jazz, who practically swooned on the spot.

Danni needn't have worried about Jazz taking notes: she was taking notes on every single time Danni breathed. I grinned, bracing myself for many Danni-wannabe moments to come from my star-struck best friend.

Jazz's Notes on Danny

Must have candy and ice-cold
Coke at all times 🍬

262

Kitten's Got Talent!

Likes to sit on left in back of limo

Favourite colour is silver-grey
(it's the new black)

Calls everyone "chick"

Does NOT like sausages

Must have a supply of fresh Minty
Chewing-gum at all times

Likes cats but not dogs

A couple of weeks ago, when we weren't speaking, Jazz would have given every pair of trainers she possessed (even the ones with rainbow-coloured laces) to be here without me, scurrying around after celebrities, and she wouldn't have missed me one bit. But that day I knew she was pleased to have me with her. 'This is all down to you and your kitten,' she whispered, squeezing my arm, once we'd left the limo.

In fact, the only thing that threatened to be a problem was Jaffa. She was in danger of blowing all the good vibes out of the window when I told her she had to sit in a cat box for a while.

'Me not like this!' she whined at me through the door. 'Me hate bein' shut in – Bertie know that. Ber-tiiiiiiie!'

'Wow! Jaffa's making a racket,' Dad said, peering in through the metal grille. 'It's all right, little Jaffsie. We'll let you out for a cuddle in a minute.'

'Me *not* want cuddles,' Jaffa mewled. 'Me want go hooooooome.'

'We'll go home the minute this is all finished, I promise,' I told her. 'You just have to sit tight and look beautiful and it'll all be worth it. Can't have you missing your moment of fame, can we?'

'OK,' Jaffa agreed, growling slightly.

Dad looked at me funnily.

'What?' I said, eyes wide and innocent.

'You and cats – I don't know. Anyone would think you two understood each other.' He smiled and patted my shoulder. 'Come to think of it . . .' he hesitated. 'It was like that with Fenella's cat as well—'

'I just think humans shouldn't talk down to animals,' I said hastily. 'They have feelings too.'

Dad shook his head, smiling wryly. 'Bertie Fletcher, you are a mystery to me.' He gave me a squeeze. 'I'm proud of you, helping set this up. If your mum could see you now . . .' He tailed off, a cloud passing over his face. I gave him a quick hug back and he pulled himself together. 'You'd better get on,' he said quietly, and pushed me gently in Fiona's direction.

The woman was a legend! She had managed to rustle up hordes of animals. There were more dogs than anything else, but I spotted a lizard and a tortoise among the crowds and something that looked like a fat squirrel, but which Fergus told me was a chinchilla. No snakes, I was pleased to see.

Fiona had arranged for all the dogs to have a separate part of the theatre to themselves. I had a sneaking suspicion Fergus had had a part in this, since seeing how worried I'd been about those spaniels.

'We don't want the bigger animals frightening the smaller ones,' Fiona told me. 'Especially not the gorgeous little puss-cats,' she said, bending down to talk to Jaffa.

So Mr Bruce's spaniels were kept as far away from Jaffa as possible, thankfully. I spotted him out of the corner of my eye, chatting to 'Bex'. Dad was hovering in the background, a bit like an over-eager puppy himself. I was glad I had enough to think about without worrying about my dad's love life. (Eeeeeuuuuuwwww!)

Fiona had organized for a semicircle of tables to be laid out for the smaller animals' cages and boxes.

I was just finishing off my tour of duty, making sure there was water and snacks for the pets, when I saw Mr Smythe arrive with Houdini and Mr Nibbles in what he called their 'travelling cage'. I went to greet him.

He immediately started chattering nervously at top speed with much nose- and moustache-twitching and polishing of glasses. 'I couldn't bring the full-size cage as it was too unwieldy. But Houdini has more than enough room in here to perform his prize-winning act,' he assured me. 'And Mr Nibbles needs no more than a little tub of sun-flower seeds to show off his particular talent.'

I smiled, thinking he sounded more nervous than I was.

'I hadn't realized *rodents* were capable of perform-ing,' Fiona said with a shudder, when I introduced her.

'Oh yes,' Mr Smythe had said chirpily, oblivious to Fiona's distaste. 'I think you will be surprised to

267

see what a hamster can do with a peanut.'

'I'm sure,' Fiona had said, grimacing.

Ty arrived looking thoroughly awestruck and clutching a ruffled, squeaky Huckleberry.

I went over to him and gave him a hug. 'Hey, Ty! Have you got a cage for Huckleberry?'

He nodded dumbly, gazing around at the mayhem, his eyes wide.

I chuckled. 'I've never seen you lost for words before!' I teased. 'Don't worry – it's going to be fun. And Huckleberry's bound to win a prize for squeakiest pet, if nothing else.' Ty grinned gratefully and put Huckleberry back in the box his mum had brought for him.

The cameras had started rolling as soon as the crowds of spectators and contestants began arriving. Fiona had said she wanted it all on film. 'I want to get a real flavour of the whole event,' she gushed. 'We want to see the public mingling with the celebs.' She pronounced it 'slebs'. 'We need a sense of the excitement building.'

She'd arranged for a telephone voting system to be put in place so that viewers at home could vote for their favourite pet, and the proceeds from the cost of the votes were definitely going to the Cats and Dogs Home.

'I didn't think your mum was serious about that,' I told Fergus, grinning like a loon.

'Oh yeah, like I said, she's crazy about cats,' he assured me. But I couldn't help thinking that he'd made sure Fiona had stuck to that part of the deal.

Once all the contestants had arrived, filming of the individual pets and their particular talents started in earnest. Jazz was there in every shot, walking behind Simon and Danni, carrying clipboards, pens, glasses of water – anything they wanted. She would have found them a flying pig if they'd asked for it. She was in her element, her chocolate-drop eyes shining and her face split into a permanent, extra-wide cherry lipgloss flavoured grin. It made my face ache with happiness just to look at her.

And then my own personal moment of glory came when the cameras came to me and Jaffa.

Danni and Simon walked over. My hands were shaking and I wasn't sure I'd be able to find my voice.

'So who's this little cutie?' Danni cooed, leaning in and beaming at Jaffa.

'Wow! I'm impressed,' said Simon, in that dead-pan way of his. 'I didn't expect to be, but – I am.'

Jaffa sat up on her haunches, looked directly at the camera and the two celebrity judges, and let out a long, high-pitched mew.

'This my best side!' she said, preening herself and blinking at the film crew.

I giggled and felt my shoulders relax. My kitten was fluttering her eyelashes! She was flirting with the camera!

Simon and Danni bent down to get a closer look.

'Oh, my!' Danni cried, reaching out her hand to give Jaffa a tickle behind the ear. 'This is absolutely the most gorgeous little kitten I have ever seen! Look at those ice-blue eyes! And that stunning fur! Oh, it's so unusual to see a ginger female cat, you know,' she added knowledgeably to Simon. 'Awwwww! She's so friendly and chatty too,' she gushed, as Jaffa rubbed her head against Danni's hand and purred loudly. 'Definitely a 'yes' from me,' Danni concluded.

'This pretty lady say all the right things to Jaffsie!' she crooned.

My eyes felt hot. I bit down hard on my lip. I was not going to lose it in front of the cameras, like those nutters in the auditions for *WGT*?

Jazz was leaping up and down behind me, grinning from ear to pierced ear, her beads jangling in her hair. 'That's my mate!' she was whooping. 'MY BEST MATE!'

Simon had actually gone gooey-eyed. 'I am not

usually a cat person, Danni, as you know. But I have to say, you're right. This little beauty has buckets of personality! It's a 'yes' from me.'

The crowd clapped and cheered and Fergus gave me a double thumbs-up sign. If Jaffa could have bowed, I'm sure she would have. As for me, I was the proudest pet-owner on the planet.

Epilogue
Kitten Smitten

Later that night, Jazz, Dad, Jaffa and I went over to the Meerleys to wait for the votes to be counted. Fiona had laid on drinks in posh, tall glasses, and there were huge bowls of yummy crisps and dips and plates piled high with mini cupcakes. Dad was soon jabbering away to Fiona about his writing while Mr Meerley ran in and out of the kitchen, topping up people's drinks and handing round snacks. Fergus, Jazz and I were huddled on one of the pristine white sofas with Jaffa curled up next to us. We were glued to the TV screen where Simon and Danni were reading out the results of the talent show and commenting on the voting.

273

When the final vote came in, it looked as though the nation had agreed with Simon and Danni – Jaffa had won!

'Well, isn't that marvellous, Berry?' Fiona trilled.

'BERTIE!' we chorused.

Fiona flushed. 'That's what I said!'

Everyone laughed.

'What you laughin' at?' Jaffa mewed.

'Shh,' I whispered. 'I'll tell you later.'

Jazz was giving me funny looks. 'Are you talking to your cat again, Bertie?' she asked, scooping up a handful of tortilla chips with her ultra-long purple talons and stuffing them into her mouth.

'Tell meeee!' Jaffa mewed.

'It seems, little Jaffa Cake, that not only are you the cutest kitten in the whole world, but you are also the cleverest,' I told her.

'Yeah,' said Fergus, ruffling her head. 'And Bertie's not the only one to think so. The whole country agreed.'

Fiona stared into her drink and muttered, 'I *am* sorry for encouraging her to come over to ours.' She looked as though she was suffering from an attack of acute indigestion. I had the feeling 'sorry' was not a word that was often heard coming from Fiona Meerley's mouth.

'That's OK,' I said with feeling. 'If you hadn't, we wouldn't all be here tonight.'

'No, it was wrong of me, Bertie.' (She got my name right!) 'I promise I won't do it again. I can see how much she means to you and how upset you were about her running away. But the fact is, Bertie,' she paused and looked at Jaffa soppily, 'it is very difficult *not* to fall for her charms.'

Fergus leaned in and said quietly, 'A bit like her owner, you could say.'

I looked awkwardly away, but not before I'd caught Jazz raising an eyebrow at me in a woooo-what-about-that! gesture that made me cringe with embarrassment.

Luckily Jaffa broke the tension by miaowing so loudly, everyone laughed.

'I think Jaffa agrees with you, Fiona!' Dad said.

'Yeah, Bertie. You gotta admit it, everyone is well and truly smitten with me!'

I had to laugh too and, cradling my kitten in my arms, I cooed, 'You never spoke a truer word, little Jaffsie.'

Collect them all!

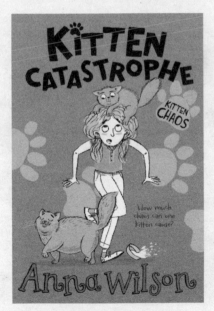

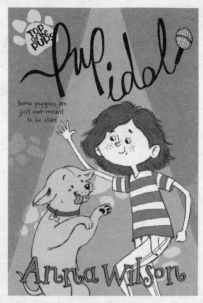

Collect them all!

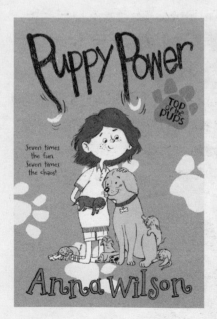

THE GREAT KITTEN
CAKE OFF

Anna Wilson

'READY? STEADY?
WHAT ARE YOU WAITING FOR? . . . BAKE!'

Ellie Haines despairs of her family. Her brother is obsessed with getting on TV, Mum is going through some kind of midlife crisis, and Dad's bad 'yolks' have reached alarming 'egg-stremes'.

The only bright spots in Ellie's life are her naughty kitten, Kitkat, and her best mate, Mads. But when Mads and Ellie apply for The Junior Cake Off, their friendship soon starts to crumble. Can Ellie win back her best mate, or will their friendship go up in smoke?

Do you love animals too?

If so I'd love to hear from you. Write to me at:

ANNA WILSON
C/O MACMILLAN CHILDREN'S BOOKS
20 NEW WHARF ROAD
LONDON N1 9RR
UNITED KINGDOM

Remember to enclose your full name and postal address (not your email address) so that I know where to write back to! And please do not send me any photos or drawings unless you are happy for me to keep them.

Anna xxx